KU-629-857

Praise for LAURIE HALSE ANDERSON

"Does *anyone* write troubled teen characters with the realism, grace, and soul of Laurie Halse Anderson?" Jodi Picoult, bestselling author of *MY SISTER'S KEEPER*

"With her trademark hope, humor, and heart-breaking realism, Laurie Halse Anderson has given us a roadmap to heal. She is a treasure" Stephen Chbosky, bestselling author of *THE PERKS OF BEING A WALLFLOWER*

Praise for PROM

"[Readers] will love Ashley's clear view of high-school hypocrisies, dating and the fierce bonds of friendship" BOOKLIST

"This book will delight readers who want their realism tempered with fun" SCHOOL LIBRARY JOURNAL

"Few adolescent girls will be able to resist Anderson's modern fairy tale" THE HORN BOOK

Praise for WINTERGIRLS

"Brilliant, intoxicating, full of drama, love and, like the best books of this kind, hope" Melvin Burgess, OBSERVER

"A fearless, riveting account of a young woman in the grip of a deadly illness" NEW YORK TIMES

"As difficult as reading this novel can be, it is even more difficult to put down" PUBLISHERS WEEKLY

"Anderson illuminates a dark but utterly realistic world ... this is necessary reading" BOOKLIST

Praise for TWISTED

"Anderson returns to weightier issues ... and stretches her wings by offering up a male protagonist for the first time" KIRKUS REVIEWS *Starred Review*

"Tyler truly suffers and the reader suffers with him ... an excellent source of both entertainment and serious conversation" KLIATT *Starred Review*

"Once again, Anderson's taut, confident writing will cause this story to linger long after the book is set down" SCHOOL LIBRARY JOURNAL

Praise for CATALYST

"Anderson excels in conveying Kate's anxieties ... the universal obstacles she faces and the realistic outcome will likely hold readers' attention" PUBLISHERS WEEKLY

"Intelligently written with multi-dimensional characters that replay in one's mind" KIRKUS REVIEWS

LAURIE HALSE ANDERSON has been published to huge critical acclaim in the United States. Known for tackling tough subjects with humour and sensitivity, her work has earned numerous awards. Two of her books, SPEAK and CHAINS, were National Book Award finalists. CHAINS was also shortlisted for the CILIP Carnegie Medal in the UK. In 2009, Laurie was honoured with the Margaret A. Edwards Award, given by YALSA division of the American Library Association for her "significant and lasting contribution to young adult literature". Mother of four and wife of one, Laurie lives in Northern New York, where she likes to watch the snow fall as she writes.

Visit her at www.madwomanintheforest.com

Also by Laurie Halse Anderson

Wintergirls
Catalyst
Prom
Chains
Forge
Speak
Fever 1793

Coming soon
The Impossible Knife of Memory

TWISTED

LAURIE HALSE ANDERSON

SCHOLASTIC

Scholastic Children's Books
An imprint of Scholastic Ltd
Euston House, 24 Eversholt Street
London, NW1 1DB, UK
Registered office: Westfield Road, Southam, Warwickshire, CV47 0RA
SCHOLASTIC and associated logos are trademarks and/or registered trademarks
of Scholastic Inc.

First published in the US by Viking, a member of Penguin Group (USA) Inc, 2007
This edition published in the UK by Scholastic Ltd, 2014

Copyright © Laurie Halse Anderson, 2007
Cover illustration copyright © Gary Newman represented by New Division, 2014

The right of Laurie Halse Anderson to be identified as the author of this work
has been asserted by her.

ISBN 978 1407 13860 2

A CIP catalogue record for this book is available from the British Library.

All rights reserved.
This book is sold subject to the condition that it shall not, by way of trade or
otherwise, be lent, hired out or otherwise circulated in any form of binding or
cover other than that in which it is published. No part of this publication may be
reproduced, stored in a retrieval system, or transmitted in any form or by any
means (electronic, mechanical, photocopying, recording or otherwise) without the
prior written permission of Scholastic Limited.

Printed and bound by CPI Group (UK) Ltd, Croydon, CRO 4YY
Papers used by Scholastic Children's Books are made from wood grown in
sustainable forests.

1 3 5 7 9 10 8 6 4 2

This is a work of fiction. Names, characters, places, incidents and dialogues are
products of the author's imagination or are used fictitiously. Any resemblance to
actual people, living or dead, events or locales is entirely coincidental.

www.scholastic.co.uk

To Scot,
for building the best fort ever

I spent the last Friday of summer vacation spreading hot, sticky tar across the roof of George Washington High. My companions were Dopey, Toothless, and Joe, the brain surgeons in charge of building maintenance. At least they were getting paid. I was working forty feet above the ground, breathing in sulphur fumes from Satan's vomitorium, for free.

Character building, my father said.

Mandatory community service, the judge said. Court-ordered restitution for the Foul Deed. He nailed me with the bill for the damage I had done, which meant I had to sell my car and bust my hump at a landscaping company all summer. Oh, and he gave me six months of meetings with a probation officer who thought I was a waste of human flesh.

Still, it was better than jail.

I pushed the mop back and forth, trying to coat the seams evenly. We didn't want any rain getting into the building and destroying the classrooms. Didn't want to hurt the school. No, sir, we sure didn't.

Joe wandered over, looked at my work, and grunted.

"We done yet?" asked Dopey. "Thunderstorms rolling in soon. Heavy weather."

I looked up. There were no clouds in the sky.

Joe nodded slowly, studying the roof. "Yeah, we're done." He turned off the motor on the tar kettle. "Last day for Tyler, here. Bet you're glad to be quit of us, huh, kid?"

"Nah," I lied. "You guys have been great."

Dopey cackled. "If the sewer pipes back up again, we'll get you out of class."

There had been a few advantages to working with these guys. They taught me how to steal soda out of the vending machines. I snagged a couple of keys when they weren't looking. Best of all, the hard labour had turned me from Nerd Boy into Tyler the Amazing Hulk, with ripped muscles and enough testosterone to power a nuclear generator.

"Hey, get a load of this!" Toothless shouted.

We picked our way around the fresh tar patches and looked where he was pointing, four stories down. I stayed away from the edge; I wasn't so good at heights. But then I saw them: angels with ponytails gathered in the parking lot.

The girls' tennis team.

Wearing bikini tops and short shorts.

Wearing wet bikini tops and wet short shorts.

I inched closer. It was a car wash, with vehicles lined up all the way out to the road, mostly driven by guys. Barely clad girls were bending, stretching, soaping up, scrubbing, and squealing. They were squirting each other with hoses. And squealing. Did I mention that?

"Take me now, Lord," Toothless muttered.

2

The marching band was practising in the teachers' lot. They fired up their version of "Louie, Louie." Finely toned tennis-angel butts bounced back and forth to the beat. Then a goddess rose up from the hubcap of a white Ford Explorer.

Bethany Milbury.

The driver of the Explorer said something. Bethany smiled and blew at the soapsuds in her hands so bubbles floated through the air and landed on his nose. The driver melted into a puddle on the front seat. Bethany threw back her head and laughed. The sun flashed off her teeth.

Joe's tongue dropped out of his mouth and sizzled on the hot roof. Dopey took off his glasses, rubbed them on a corner of his shirt, and put them back on. Toothless adjusted himself.

Bethany bounced along to the next car in line, a dark-green Avenger that was burning oil.

Bethany Milbury pushes me against the hood of my cherry-red, turbocharged Testarossa. "I love fast cars," she whispers, soapy fingers in my hair.

"This is the fastest," I say.

"I've been waiting so long for you, Tyler..." Her head tilts, her lips open.

I am so ready for this.

She grabs my arm and snarls, "Be careful, dummy, you'll break your neck."

No, wait. I blinked. I was on a hot tar roof with three smelly grown men. Joe was gripping my arm, yanking me back from the edge.

3

"I said, be careful, dummy. That first step is a doozy."

"Sorry," I said. "I mean, thanks."

A navy-blue 1995 Mercedes S500 sedan rolled into the parking lot. It came to a complete stop. Left blinker flashing, it turned and parked in front of the building. A man in a black suit got out of the driver's seat. Stood next to the car. Looked up at me and tapped the face of his watch once, twice, three times. I had inconvenienced him again.

Dopey, Toothless, and Joe crawled out of sight. They had seen my father detonate before.

2.

On the public-humiliation scale, being picked up in Dad's car was better than being picked up in Mom's. Yes, it had a couple rust spots and 162,000 miles on it, but at least it was a Benz. Mom drove an ancient Suburban, beige, dented from encounters with mailboxes and trees. If I had my own car back, that would've been the best.

When I came out the front door, he pointed to the trunk, gaping open.

I stripped off my sweatshirt, boots, and wet socks, and dumped them in the cardboard box stuck in a nest of investment brochures and bungee cords. I left my jeans on. Even Dad knew it would not be cool to strip down to my boxers in front of the school.

"Hurry up," he called.

I sat on the beach towel laid on the backseat. Wouldn't want to mess up the leather.

His cell phone rang. His lip curled slightly when he saw the number on the screen. He answered the phone. "What is it now?"

Meet my father: Corporate Tool. He'd always been a hardass, but since his latest promotion, he'd dialled it up.

"That's not my problem," he told the phone. "It's yours. Solve it."

Mom stared at him from the passenger seat, then sighed deeply. It was Friday afternoon, which meant they had just come from their therapy session. They were recovering the joy in their relationship.

"Hi, Mom," I said.

She looked back and gave me a little wave. Her smile was fake, like a piece of paper with a smile drawn on it had been glued to her face.

As I buckled my seat belt, Dad ended his call and started the engine. "I still don't know why you insist on picking him up every day," he told Mom. "It wouldn't kill him to ride his bike."

Mom's smile fell off. She blinked hard and studied the dust on the dashboard.

Meet my mother: pet photographer, cake baker, nice lady who smells faintly of gin.

Dad put the car in reverse and glanced at me in the mirror.

"We have an office barbecue tonight," he said. "I suppose it's too late for you to get a haircut before then."

I shook my bangs in front of my eyes. "I don't want to go."

"I expect you and your sister to be ready by seven o'clock."

"I have plans," I said, which was not exactly true, but sounded good.

"Change them." Dad looked beyond me. "Dammit."

We were blocked in by the cars lined up to be washed. Dad shifted back into park and turned off the engine. "Don't want to waste gas," he muttered. His phone rang again. He answered it without a word, listened for a moment, then launched into a rant about federal regulations and inter-office memos.

Mom rolled down her window and waved at one of the tennis players soaping up a Volvo. She waved at Bethany Milbury. *The* Bethany Milbury. Bethany waved back.

I thought the tar fumes had made me delusional. She'd been in my homeroom since seventh grade. She'd had the starring role in most of my fantasies since then, too.

But this was real.

Bethany Milbury, Holy Goddess of Hotness, floated … towards … our car. She put her clean hands with their perfect fingernails on my mother's door and leaned forward, straining the top of her bikini to the max.

"Hey, Tyler," Bethany said to me.

I had this weird rushing noise in my ears. My jeans tightened near the zipper.

"Ha," I said. "Heya-ha."

Idiot. Moron. Cretin. Fool.

Mom said something about the party. Bethany looked surprised for a second, but then Mom mentioned pasta salad and I stopped listening because a drop of water slipped from Bethany's collarbone to her cleavage. I leaned forward for a better view of the water crawling, millimeter by millimeter, down the golden, soft canyon of her . . .

"Ow!"

Both Mom and Bethany stopped talking to stare at me.

"Did you hit your head, Tyler?" Mom asked.

"Are you OK?" Bethany asked.

"Ha," I said.

As we pulled out of the parking lot, I pressed my face against the back window to watch her walk away. Bethany was the Alpha Female of George Washington High – the most beautiful, the most popular, the queen bee. She was also the daughter of my dad's boss, and the sister of the guy who had been making my life hell for years.

And me? I was a zit on the butt of the student body. I had a screwed-up past and no visible future. My chances of hooking up with anything female, much less Bethany, were small.

But anything was possible on the last Friday of summer vacation.

The Milburys lived in the Hampton Club and Estates, ten blocks and fifty million miles away from our house. It was close enough to walk to, and far enough that we should have chartered a jet. My parents were struggling wannabes of the upper middle class. The Milburys were the people they wanted to be.

"I can't believe you're making us do this," Hannah bitched as we pulled out of our driveway at precisely seven p.m. "Why can't we stay home?"

Mom balanced a two-gallon plastic bowl of pasta salad in her lap. "Don't whine."

"I'm not whining."

Dad slowed down to go around a pothole. "You're whining about not whining."

"How can you say that?" Hannah asked.

"In English," Dad said. "So you should be able to understand it."

"Enough," Mom said. "We're going to a party. Can't we have some fun?"

Dad cleared his throat. "This is not 'a party'," he corrected. "It's a business function. We're going to put in a family appearance, I need ten minutes of face time with Brice, and then we can leave. I expect everyone to be on their best behaviour."

His eyes found mine in the rearview mirror. "Including you."

*

Dad liked to pretend I was a dangerous criminal because of the Foul Deed. But it was just a stupid prank. I mean, all pranks are stupid, but that's kind of the point, isn't it?

The last time anybody had noticed me (in a good way) was in third grade when I won the home-run contest during Field Day. After that, my reputation struck out every time. I was the shortest guy in middle school and too chicken to hit back. I had "victim" tattooed on my forehead.

It got a little better in high school. I became invisible, your average piece of drywall who spent too much time playing computer games. Girls would look straight at me and never see the writhing masculine beast hidden inside my hundred thirty-five pounds of veal-white man-flesh. So at the end of my junior year, I decided to do something bold. A prank that would turn me into a legend.

At three o'clock in the morning on Monday, May first, I used five cans of spray paint to decorate George Washington High with words that proclaimed the superiority of the junior class and a couple of crude remarks about the manhood of Principal Hughes.

I misspelled "phenomenal" and "testicle." I also forgot one of the cans, the red one. And I was so flustered, trying to finish before the sun came up, that I didn't notice my wallet was missing until the police arrived on our front porch.

"Best behaviour," Dad repeated. "Be an asset, not a liability."

Hannah made a face at the back of his pointy head.

I stared at him in the mirror until he looked away.

4.

The Milburys' house was what you'd expect: monstrously big and slightly tacky.

"It's gorgeous!" Mom said. "So tasteful. What a beautiful fountain."

Dad muttered something under his breath. He wiped the sweat off his forehead with the back of his hand.

Wisps of barbecue smoke and jazz drifted from the backyard. We came to a screeching halt as we rounded the corner of the house.

"Whoa," Hannah said.

Yeah.

A massive swimming pool, complete with hot tub and waterfall, took up a third of the yard and was ringed with a broad patio and burning tiki torches. A jazz quartet was playing at the far end, close to the bar. Right in front of us were two tented pavilions, one for food and one filled with tables and chairs. A pig was roasting on a giant spit, and a cook was slapping down hamburgers on a grill. Waiters buzzed around with trays of snack food, glasses of wine, and imported beer in dark bottles. The golf course (a Hampton Estates perk) stretched out beyond the rose garden.

The place was packed: people standing, sitting, eating, drinking, dancing, flirting, frowning, laughing, practising pretend golf swings, and watching each other. It was mostly adults, but the hot tub was filled with half of the lacrosse team, and a couple of other kids from school were scattered around the patio. The rich kids, the really rich kids. You know what they look like.

Mom yanked Dad out of view. "How could you do this to me?" she hissed. "This isn't 'casual' and it is absolutely not potluck."

Dad frowned. "The memo said casual. Casual means potluck. Everybody knows that."

"Memo?" Mom's voice went up. "What memo? You said Brice invited you personally."

"Be quiet," Dad said. "Here comes Doreen."

Mom handed the pasta salad to Hannah, who turned and handed it to me.

"Get rid of it," Mom whispered.

I bent down and stuck the bowl behind a bush. When I stood up, Bethany and her mom were talking to my parents. Bethany was wearing a long Hawaiian-skirt thing tied around her hips and a see-through lace shirt over her bikini top. The peanut butter-coloured cat she was carrying obstructed my view. Mrs Milbury was an older and thinner version of her daughter, with a tan that made her skin look like a tired leather sofa, and very large, very white teeth.

Mrs Milbury gave me the once-over. "My goodness,

Tyler," she said. "You used to be four-foot-nothing and skinny as a beanpole. You certainly have grown up."

"He's six-three and one ninety-five," Mom said. "Growing taller every day, like a cornstalk!"

Hannah snorted.

"Ah," I said, cringing. "Ha."

Dad tapped his foot and waited a suave two seconds before he blurted out, "So, where's Brice?"

5.

Brice Milbury, CEO of Milbury Brothers Trust ("Trust Milbury Trust!"), was the tall man with the perfect tan and fat gold watch motioning to Mrs Milbury from the far side of the pool. Three shorter guys were grouped behind him, all wearing lime-green golf shirts with the company logo. As we walked up, his son Chip did, too. Chip Milbury: Bethany's evil twin brother, four-year lacrosse starter, fairly good offensive linebacker, and all-American jerk who majored in beating the crap out of me in middle school.

We did more of the fake-polite handshaking thing. Mr Milbury held on to Dad's hand an extra moment. "Surprised to see you here, Bill," he said. "Didn't know your department was coming."

The short dweeb guys looked at each other. I knew in the pit of my stomach that Dad had screwed up. You didn't crash parties in Hampton Estates, even if you were the new Vice President of Oversight and Compliance. Not cool.

Dad gripped his boss's hand harder. "You know me, Brice, always looking out for the company's best interests."

(Yeah, he said that.)

"So, Nerd Boy." Chip punched me in the shoulder. Hard. "They let you work out in prison?"

"Tyler didn't go to prison—" Mom shut her mouth when Dad shook his head once.

Mr Milbury looked me over. "You playing football, Tyler?"

"No, sir," I said. "I've just been working."

"Part of his parole," Chip said.

"My job," I said slowly. "I work at Pirelli's Landscaping."

Mr Milbury squeezed my bicep. "Maybe you should do some manual labour, Chip. This guy's made of steel."

Chip stood up straight, trying to make himself as tall as me. "How much can you press?"

"I have no idea." *Two fifty-pound sacks of mulch in each hand, douche bag.*

"You two boys should work out together," Mr Milbury said. "Looks like you'd be a good match."

"We're not matched," Chip said.

The band broke into "La Macarena." A few women jumped out of their seats, formed a line at the edge of the pool, and flailed their arms around. Mom and Mrs Milbury both wiggled their hips. Hannah slunk off towards the food tent.

Bethany managed to look incredibly bored and incredibly hot at the same time.

"You could bring Tyler to the gym," Mr Milbury suggested to Dad. "I'll meet you there with Chip. We're always looking for someone to push him to the next level."

Chip blinked fast and pretended to watch the pig turning on the spit.

"That would be great," Dad said. "I'll tell Linda. Now, if I could just borrow you for a few minutes, Brice. The situation in Omaha is uglier than I thought. The new regulations. . ."

One of the dweebs whispered something into Mr Milbury's ear. Dad snapped his mouth shut and tried not to frown.

"This isn't the place for business. You can call Stuart here on Monday," Mr Milbury said. "We'll set up a meeting." He turned away from my father and patted my shoulder. "I don't know, Chipper. I think Tyler might be out of your league."

"Let's find out." Chip sat down at a small table and placed his elbow square in the middle, palm open. "What do you say, Tyler? Think you can take me?"

"Knock it off, Chip," Bethany said.

"Chicken?" Chip asked.

"Great idea," Mr Milbury said. "I'll bet you a round of golf, Bill. Your boy against mine. What do you say? You golf, don't you?"

"*Braaaaawck*," Chip clucked softly.

14

"I love golf," Dad lied. "Go ahead, Tyler."

"All right." I sat down across from Chip and planted my right elbow next to his.

A crowd quickly gathered around our table. He wiggled his fingers, then grabbed my hand. I let him squeeze without fighting back. The left corner of his mouth twisted up in a half-grin.

There were no calluses on his palms.

"This won't take long," Chip told his buddies.

"On my count," Mr Milbury said. "Start on 'three.'"

Chip opened his hand and regripped. This time I squeezed before he did. He blinked.

"One," Mr Milbury said. The band played "La Macarena" faster.

"Two.

"Th—"

Chip didn't wait for his father to finish the word. I didn't think he would. I was ready. When he pushed, my forearm hardened into a steel girder planted in cement. Chip frowned when my arm didn't budge. He took a deep breath and tried to curl his hand over mine. I drove it back and tested the strength of his arm. He had nothing on me.

The lacrosse guys yelled at Chip to put me away. Chip glanced up at his father.

I kept staring straight at him.

Our arms were shaking, making the table wobble on the uneven slate. Chip was breathing harder. I could smell the pizza he ate, the beer he drank, and the Tic Tacs he used to cover them up.

Mr Milbury stepped closer to the table. "Looks like we have ourselves a draw, folks!"

"No, we don't," Chip said.

My father moved behind his boss, pretending he wanted a better angle to watch.

"Want to quit?" I asked.

"Shut up," Chip said.

The song ended.

"Do it, Tyler!" Bethany said.

Boiling blood filled my arm, white-hot with strength.

"Do it!"

Staring dead into Chip's eyes, I powered his arm backwards one inch. Another inch. I could see how this was going to end. I would take him down smoothly, pushing his hand to the tabletop and forcing him out of his seat so his shoulder wouldn't be ripped from the socket.

And then I made the mistake of looking at Dad.

He shook his head, just a little bit, from side to side.

I closed my eyes and let my enemy win.

6.

Chip leaped up, balled his fists, and screamed, "Yeah!"

The crowd around us fell silent. A couple of lacrosse players congratulated Chip and jumped in the pool. The dweebs reached for new beers. Mrs Milbury drifted towards the band. Dad watched the guys in the water. Bethany was the only person who looked me in the eye.

"Good job, fair fight," said Mr Milbury. "He almost had you there, Chipper. Better watch your back! Ha-ha. Now shake hands like men."

Chip ignored his father and shadowboxed one of his henchmen, a kid named Parker with perfect teeth and acne scars.

"Chipper," Mr Milbury repeated, a little louder.

The last thing Chip wanted to do was shake my hand. Instead, he shoved Parker, who backpedalled and fell into the pool, hitting the water with a loud smack.

"Son!" Mr Milbury's voice snapped through the air like a wet towel in a locker room.

Chip froze for a second, then walked back to me, his hand extended. "Fair fight," he said.

"Something like that," I said. I smiled and squeezed his hand until the bones rubbed together like dry twigs. He grunted and covered his pain with a cough. I kept squeezing.

Mr Milbury had no clue. He patted me on the back. "Maybe we should have Tyler do our landscaping," he said. "I bet he'd work faster than those illegals Doreen is always hiring."

"Sure thing, Mr Milbury," I said, releasing Chip's hand.

Dad stepped forward. "Brice, I don't think this can wait until Monday. If we could sit down for a few minutes. . ."

17

"Ah, time for a toast." Waiters were hurrying through the crowd passing out champagne. At the microphone, Mrs Milbury tapped her glass with a spoon.

"Have a drink, Bill," Mr Milbury said, waving over a waiter. "Whatever the problem is, I know you'll fix it. Relax. Enjoy being out with the family."

One of the dweebs snickered. That's why I wasn't ready.

Chip reached out and patted me on the back, like his father had. But instead of a friendly pat, he smacked me as hard as he could. The blow sent me flying towards Bethany and the waiters loaded with champagne trays.

The world downshifted to slow motion.

The waiters stumbled, and their trays flew up. Bethany stepped backwards, then fell. My arms tried to catch her. My legs fought for balance. All the dads and dweebs stood, frozen, mouths open. The trays came down, and fifty champagne glasses hit the patio.

A million shards of glass and champagne exploded.

Bethany screamed.

As time sped up, just before I hit the ground, I noticed one more thing.

Bethany was barefoot.

She screamed again.

We went down in a heap speckled with glass and blood. Chip vanished into the roses.

Half of the Milbury Brothers Trust's board of directors were doctors. By the time the ambulance arrived, they'd stopped the bleeding and taken out most of the glass, but Bethany needed a shot and stitches in the bottom of her left foot.

The ambulance left, lights flashing, no sirens.

My mom retrieved her pasta salad from the bushes and put it in the car. Then she came back and patted my hand while one of the doctors looked me over and patched me up with a half dozen butterfly bandages. Hannah stayed next to me.

Dad had disappeared. We finally found him practising spin control with his boss, trying to convince Mr Milbury to sue the company that laid the slate around the pool because they clearly did a shoddy job, which had led to such dangerous conditions and the unfortunate accident.

Before we left, I found one of the doctors who had helped me and quietly asked him to slit my throat.

The guy said no and suggested I talk to my family doc about antidepressants.

I spent most of Friday night playing Tophet. The graphics weren't that great and it made my computer freeze regularly, but it was better than lying awake and loathing myself for hurting Bethany.

Tophet was Hell. The point of the game was to make your demon as powerful as possible and survive through the sixty-six Levels of Torment. After that, I wasn't sure what would happen. Either he'd escape to Heaven or descend to the Final Pit and be crowned Lord of Darkness. It was unclear which option was better.

As soon as I opened the game, a herd of fallen angels swarmed my demon, Gormley. They tied him up and stuck him in one of the boiling cauldrons. It took forever to annihilate them. My fingers hit the buttons in the right sequence over and over. It normally sounded cool when he scored a kill – lots of hissing and yowling – but I had to keep it down so Dad didn't hear me playing.

See, that was why I was a bad son. Lack of respect.

Miller men were disciplined. Miller men followed rules. Miller men toughed it out; they ate dirt and went for the kill.

That last one was a real quote. Dad said it to me when I was eleven, after I lost the Little League championship. The ball had been hit square to the shortstop and I took too much of a lead so I was trapped between third and home. Dad screamed for me to go, so I went, and I slid and was tagged by the catcher.

Grandpa Miller told Dad I was a pansy for not taking out the catcher's legs and I didn't want it bad enough and Dad agreed with him. Mom lost it in a very controlled way and told them they were both lunatics. She dragged me and Hannah home so I missed going with the team for hot dogs after the game.

I got stuck on Level Forty-Two. Gormley couldn't get past the sulphur pits. Every time I tried to teach him how to swim, he drowned.

Stupid demon.

I made a note to myself to look for a lifejacket he could buy, swallowed four ibuprofen, and went to sleep just before three thirty.

9.

My alarm went off at five the next morning. First thought: *It was a bad dream.*

Second thought: *No, it wasn't.*

Third thought: *Crap.*

I tried to eat some potato chips for breakfast, but I couldn't choke them down. I threw a bunch of lunch stuff in a grocery bag, grabbed a gallon of iced tea out of the fridge, and headed outside.

Yoda was waiting for me on the steps, holding the lunch his mother packed for him in an insulated bag. His energy drinks were in the cooler that he was sitting on. He looked up from his comic book. "Thought you might have left the country."

Yoda wasn't his real name, of course. Calvin Hodges was renamed Yoda after he flipped about *Star Wars* in fifth grade. He spent way too much time gaming (more than me, even) and he could mind-meld hard drives. But *Star Wars*, that wasn't a geek thing for him. It was his religion. When the assholes of the world beat him up for this, he'd act like a Buddhist monk being tortured by Communist soldiers. He'd smile. Freaked them out. The Force was with him.

"You heard?" I asked.

"Everybody heard, moron." He picked up the cooler and followed me down the walk. "They heard that you went on a rampage and attacked Bethany Milbury. That you got hauled away in handcuffs again. That Bethany almost died."

"It wasn't like that at all. It was an accident. But I don't want to talk about it."

"Did you punch Chip in the mouth?"

"I'm going to punch *you* in the mouth if you don't shut up."

"All right, all right. God, you're so touchy. There's the truck."

It was a fifteen-minute ride in Mr Pirelli's pickup to Evergreen Haven, the nursing home where we sent my grandparents to die.

Pirelli gave out the assignments. The Honduran guys

were in charge of mowing. Yoda had to edge the flower beds and blow the sidewalks clean. I had to run the weed whacker and dig a hole for a blue spruce using a pick and a shovel.

"Ask your buddy for help," Pirelli said when I complained.

We both looked at Yoda slathering SPF-50 sunscreen on his arms. He was hired out of desperation after most of the regular crew went back to college.

"Good luck." The boss chuckled as he jumped into his truck.

I decapitated dandelions all morning, leaving carnage and death strewn in my path.

When Yoda whistled for our lunch break, I walked over to a white oak that would give us some decent shade. I stripped off my shirt and hung it over a branch, then poured ice water over my head and let it cut through the sweat and dirt caked around my neck.

Yoda was eating the white-bread-mayo-lettuce-bologna sandwich cut into four pieces he'd had every day since first grade. I pulled out the half loaf of bread and peanut butter and jelly jars from my grocery bag and slapped together three sandwiches which I inhaled, stopping only to guzzle iced tea. The Honduran guys found their own patch of shade to eat in.

I dumped out some Oreos and tossed the package to Yoda.

"So, like I was saying," he said as he pulled out a cookie, "everybody thinks you got busted again."

"You weren't saying anything, and we're not talking about it."

He twisted the Oreo open. "Are we talking about school?"

"Hell, no."

"How about my new Sith Lords in Congress theory?"

"Not." I looked in my bag again. I'd forgotten the Doritos.

"Can we talk about Hannah?"

I put the jars back in the bag and drained the last of the iced tea. "Friends don't date friends' sisters. It's a rule. Back to work."

"Rules are made to be broken. We've been IMing every night, you know." Yoda scraped the icing off his Oreo. "She thinks I'm 'sweet.'" He stuck the two cookie halves together and devoured them. "Look, this Bethany thing will blow over. Relax, you should."

"Shut up, Yoda."

I left my shirt hanging on the tree and went back to work.

The five-foot circumference of the hole I was supposed to dig was marked with pink spray paint. I just had to make a hole as deep as the circle was wide.

I used my boot to push the shovel blade into the dirt, bent my knees, put my back into it and lifted. Ten minutes into the work, I was sweating. Half an hour and I was dripping. After a while my cuts and bruises stopped hurting, and the whine of the edger and mowers faded away. It was just the slice of the shovel into the ground and the pounding of my heart as I muscled it out of the hole. An inch at a time, a foot at a time. I was good at digging holes. It was the rest of life I sucked at.

Then I hit rock – check that, rocks – and the dirt turned into dried cement. I had to use the pick to loosen it. The mowers swept by, blasting cut grass and exhaust. I kept digging, pick first, then shovel. Pick and shovel. Break, then dig. An inch, three inches, another foot down. The sun was roaring overhead, cooking everything. Sweat ran down my back and arms. Salt penetrated the bandages the doc had given me. The sting was sweet.

Days like this I thought maybe I should just blow off school, move to Minnesota or something, get a job that let me sweat, and never, ever think again. I swung the pick harder, putting my back into it until the sun and the stink and the buzz and the pain blurred together.

And then Yoda was standing above me with Mr Pirelli next to him. Somehow the afternoon had vanished and it was time to go home. I handed up my tools. The two of them reached down to help me out of the crater I'd dug.

"Isn't that a little deep?" Yoda asked.

"It'll help the roots get established," I explained.

"Established where? China?"

The truck stopped at our corner and we crawled out. Mr Pirelli reminded me to call him about my schedule now that school was starting. He'd take as many hours as I could give, he said, especially if I wanted to dig holes. It might have been a compliment, but I was too tired to be sure.

I trudged next to Yoda, my boots clomping on the sidewalk like monster feet.

"You want to come?" Yoda asked.

"Where?"

"To my house, to take over the galaxy, duh. Or we could just hang out. Whatever. We have leftover lasagna."

"No, I'm good. Thanks."

We stood there for a second, gnats swarming in front of our faces.

He swatted at them. "I think you should come."

"I'm OK, really," I said. "I'm going to bed. But if I can't sleep, I'll come over."

He nodded. "You riding with me Monday?"

"Nope. I'm taking the bus with Hannah."

"Cool. May the Force be with you, my friend."

"We're seniors, Yoda. You gotta stop saying that."

10.

My house was dark and quiet.

No dinner, no notes on the counter. Maybe my family had joined the witness-protection programme in exchange for testifying about what a loser I was.

I stood in the shower until the water swirling around the

drain wasn't black. Two of the butterfly bandages on my left forearm peeled off. I poured peroxide on the gaping cuts until they went numb.

When I went back down to the kitchen, I saw the thin line of light under the closed door to the basement. I filled a mixing bowl with an entire box of Lucky Charms and ate it with a serving spoon. The goal was to finish the cereal before falling asleep facedown in the milk.

After I put the bowl in the dishwasher, I opened the basement door. Dad was down there typing on his computer and talking to himself. Opera was playing low in the background.

"Tyler?" Dad called. "Is someone there? Linda?"

There had actually been a time when Dad was cool. Like when I was in third grade, when he was an accountant at a tiny hole-in-the-wall company. If you were going to make a documentary about our family, that would have been the year. Nobody had a shrink. Mom worked part-time at the school library and took photos for fun. Hannah only bit me if I made her really, really mad. And Dad and me won first place in both the father/son knot-tying competition and the three-legged race at the Cub Scout Wilderness Weekend.

Those were the days, by golly.

Now he was a dragon hiding in the skin of a small man. In public, he'd act like a human being, all handshakes and "good to meet you" and grown-up BS about the stock market and going bald. In private, the skin slid off and all you saw were slime-coloured scales and poisonous claws because a branch office was in trouble or new regulations were hurting the bottom line.

"Hello?" Dad demanded.

I closed the door.

Mom's room was to the right at the top of the staircase. Dad's was at the opposite end of the hall. Hannah and I were in the middle; her door closest to Mom's, mine next to Dad's.

I flopped on my stomach. My feet hung over the edge of the mattress.

It was the last Saturday night before my senior year of high school and I was alone in my room.

The curtains moved.

Kids were playing kickball in the street, yelling about fouls and do-overs and who was safe. Engines raced and tyres peeled out a couple blocks away. Music came from open windows. The train whistle blew. If you took the train to Cleveland, you could pick up the Capitol Limited and ride it to Chicago, and from Chicago, transfer to anywhere.

I rolled over onto my back and prayed again to every god I had ever heard of to let me die. Quick and painless. *Please.*

Death is funny, when you think about it. Everybody does it, but nobody knows how, exactly how. My Grandpa Miller just wouldn't die, no matter how sick he got. Grandma Barnett dropped dead in front of the canned vegetables at the Safeway.

Did they like it? Was it a relief?

I wasn't supposed to think about that, but it was like porn. The idea would sneak in and – *boom* – I was off. Like when they put me in the holding cell after they arrested me for the Foul Deed, and the guard came back and took the laces out of my sneakers. And then the door locked and my sneakers looked pathetic and I couldn't walk in them. And I thought about it.

As soon as it started, I'd go: *I'm not going to think about this. No matter what. I am thinking about something different now, thinking, thinking...*

And the pictures would flash over and over in my mind like a demented video with no music, just bodies falling off bridges and planes flying into skyscrapers and fires and ropes and guns and driving very fast. Unbuckling my seat belt. Aiming for the cliff at the granite quarry. Stomping the accelerator. Passing ninety when I hit the edge. Flying, then plunging to the bottom, the car bouncing off the slabs of granite, spinning, crumpling. The explosion.

Thinking about death relaxed me, as usual.

My open cuts dripped on the sheets.

Gone.

11.

I stumbled downstairs for breakfast around noon. Six fried eggs and a quart of orange juice later, I noticed a vanilla-frosted layer cake, decorated with pink rosebuds, sitting on the counter.

I reached for a knife just as Mom came around the corner. She slapped my hand. "Don't touch. It's not for us."

"Who's it for?"

"The Milburys."

"You made them a sucking-up cake?"

"This is not a 'sucking-up cake.' This is an apology cake, for Bethany's accident. The last thing this family needs is to have your father fired. So you're going to deliver it and apologize."

"No way. I won't. I can't. You don't understand, Mom – she's Bethany – she's *the* Bethany. She thinks I'm the biggest bag of sh—"

"Language!"

"—of *manure* in the whole state. I am not delivering that cake. You can't force me. Besides, it'll piss Dad off if I go over there."

"This was your father's idea, Tyler. If you don't walk this over to the Milburys this second, you'll have to deal with him."

12.

I came up with a new apology every step of the way.

Bethany, I am an idiot.

Bethany, words fail to convey the depth of my sorrow...

I am really, really, really, really...

Bethany, beautiful Bethany, wherefore art thou...

The cake was beginning to sag in the heat. *Hurry up, moron.*

After I passed through the entrance gate to the Hampton Club and Estates, I froze. I lifted the cake above my head and sniffed my pits. I should have put on more deodorant before I left. Or cologne. Did my shorts smell, too? Did the Milburys have dogs? Would they send them out to attack me? The dogs would rip off my clothes and feast on my flesh and the cake would be a sticky stain on the driveway.

I took two steps and stopped again. The visual of having my clothes ripped off in front of Bethany Milbury...

A sprinkler system kicked on.

I sprinted. Only a few drops made it to the cake, but between the heat and the water, the rosebuds were dissolving. Running caused the frosting to lean dangerously, so I slowed to a power-walk, sticking to the shady side of the street, keeping my eyes open for out-of-control sprinklers and other dangers.

I hustled up to the Milburys' door and rang the bell.

Mrs Milbury answered. She blinked once when she saw me, but then remembered her lines. "Tyler."

I held up the cake. "My mother sent this. For Bethany." She waited.

"Um, I sent it, too – am sending it, I mean. I'm the one carrying it. Um, I'm here to, you know, to see how she is. After what happened. You know. I am truly sorry, Mrs Milbury."

She took the cake from me. "Nothing to apologize for, Tyler. Those waiters had no experience and should never have worked a party like ours. It's not your fault they couldn't hold on to a tray of glasses."

OK, I was confused, but she hadn't killed me and that was all that counted. I could go home and tell Mom "mission accomplished."

"Why don't you come in and chat with Bethany?"

"Um, no, I can't. I have to be somewhere."

"On a Sunday afternoon?"

"It's, ah, Sunday school. Sunday afternoon school. Church stuff."

Her mouth dropped open in surprise. "Why, Tyler Miller, handsome and spiritual, too. You're much deeper than you look. But I'm sure the Lord won't mind if you take a few minutes to make an injured girl feel better." She narrowed her eyes until they reminded me of the business end of a rifle. "Don't you agree?"

"Yes, ma'am. Whatever you say, ma'am."

She blinked and suddenly she was Mrs Brice Milbury, society queen, again. "Follow me!"

Their front hall looked like a hotel lobby: white walls, gold-framed mirrors, a table with fake flowers stuck in a vase, and a giant staircase winding its way up to the second floor. Muzak was in the air.

She led me to the basement door and down the steps to the media room. You could have screened a movie for a dozen friends there and still had enough space for a poker tournament. The newest Sony flat screen was mounted on the wall. Actually, it took up the whole wall. The other walls were covered by framed NFL jerseys. Signed.

But I wasn't there to drool.

I was there to grovel.

Bethany was half-buried in a yellow, overstuffed chair, watching lions sleep under a tree on the TV. She was wearing a Washington Warriors tennis T-shirt and grey sweatpants rolled up to her knees, and the peanut butter coloured cat was in her lap, its tail curled around her wrist like a bracelet. Her left foot, wrapped in bandages, rested on a pillow on the coffee table. Three crutches lay in pieces on the carpet.

"What's he doing here?" she asked her mother.

"He came to cheer you up," Mrs Milbury said. "I'll just put this in the fridge."

"I don't want cheering. Make him go. Leave the cake."

Mrs Milbury shook her head. "Don't want to tempt you, sweetie. Not when you can't exercise."

"I said leave it," Bethany said louder.

I glanced around for an emergency exit.

Mrs Milbury set the tired cake on the coffee table and put her hands on her hips. "Maybe Tyler would like to sit with you

33

while I run down to Teresa's and look over their crutches. I don't want you to be alone."

"Sure thing," I said.

Bethany sighed dramatically.

Her mother wagged her finger back and forth. "Just don't eat all that cake before I get back."

I was alone with Bethany Milbury. In her basement. Was this a new pain level in Tophet or a dream? What was I supposed to do? Talk?

A male lion on the TV shook his mane and rolled on his back in the dust. The lionesses stretched and yawned as the sun set over the savanna. "They're headed out for the hunt," the voice-over explained.

Saysomethingsaysomethingsaysomethingsaysomething.

Bethany picked at the pale pink polish on her left thumbnail. Her cat sneered at me.

Say anything, you pathetic loser.

I picked up the centre post of one of the broken crutches. It had a deep crack running down it and splinters of wood bristling from one side.

"What happened to this?" I asked.

Brilliant opening! Great job!

"Chip."

"He was making firewood?"

"Fooling around with his stupid friends."

"Huh?"

Careful. Don't scare her off by grunting.

The lionesses circled a herd of gazelles at a watering hole. Bethany muted the TV. "Chip and his friends. They have a wrestling club. The crutches were props."

"Chip's on the wrestling team?"

"Club, not team. They pretend to be professional wrestlers. It's ridiculous." She held out her hand, checking her nails. The cat jumped off her lap and strutted over to me, sniffing my sneakers. "Chip's an ass," she said.

The words flew out before I could stop them. "Got that right."

"He crumpled the hood of Mom's Jag once," Bethany said. "Accidentally dropped a twenty-pound weight on it. Told Mom it happened in the grocery-store parking lot. He almost got her to sue them for damages."

"Some people get away with everything," I said.

A lioness singled out a weak gazelle. She was on it in two strides, her mouth ripping out the neck, claws dug deep in the gazelle's flesh.

Bethany watched the screen without reacting to the bloodshed. "He never gets caught." She set the remote on the arm of the chair. "I saw him push you. I tried to tell Dad, but he didn't believe me."

"Oh, man." The dam burst. "I am so sorry. I wish you knew even one-tenth of one percent of how sorry I am. It doesn't matter that Chip pushed me. It was my fault. Can I kill myself here, or should I do it outside so the mess on the carpet doesn't upset your mother?" *Grovel time*. I lay face-down on the floor in front of her chair. "Cafufowifmuh?"

"What did you say?"

I lifted my head and blew a piece of carpet fluff out of my mouth. "I said, can you forgive me? I am a moron, a loser—"

She covered her ears. "Enough! Stop! Apology accepted. The whole thing was stupid. The caterers told us to use plastic glasses, but Mom pitched a fit and insisted on the real thing. She grew up worshipping *Dallas*. Gag."

"I'm sorry. I'm sorry. I'm really, really sorry."

"Get up, Tyler."

She grabbed a handful of my T-shirt and pulled. I sat up on my knees in front of her chair. When she let go of my shirt, her hand brushed by my cheek. It smelled like soap and ice cream and girl: pure and perfect girl. Her touch set my face on fire. My face and everything else.

"Let's eat cake," she said.

The cat twitched its tail and left.

13.

Bethany sucked some frosting off her finger and moaned.

The moan woke up my trouser snake (*Down, boy! Down, I say!*) so I wandered up to the kitchen to get some forks and paper towels and room to breathe. When the snake crawled back under a rock, I went downstairs.

Bethany had switched channels to a black-and-white movie. She kept the sound muted and we took turns making up dialogue for the action on the screen. She slowly worked her way through a hunk of cake.

I couldn't eat.

This was very confusing.

I could always eat. Even when I had the flu I could eat. I'd puke, brush my teeth, and beg Mom for chips or a sandwich or French toast. But there I was in front of one of my mother's cakes (my sainted, blessed mother) and a pretty girl, and my stomach had shut down.

I switched the channel to one of the Sunday-afternoon shout-fests with plastic politicians and did play-by-play as if it were a boxing match. Bethany laughed. My stomach relaxed as if that one sound, her laughter, was what I'd been secretly hungry for my whole life.

When a commercial came on, Bethany scootched forward in her seat and tried to stand. As soon as she put pressure on her bandaged foot, she winced and fell back into her chair.

"What's wrong?" I asked. "You're in pain. That's bad. Can I help? What do you want me to do?" *Oh, God, shut up right now.* "I won't fall on you, I swear."

"Chill, Tyler. I just need to go to the bathroom."

"Here," I said, holding out my hand to her. "Let me help you."

I pulled her to her feet. She teetered a moment and clutched my arms. Her left knee was bent so her foot wouldn't touch the floor. I was six-three. She was five-six, five-seven maybe. There was no way for her to sling an arm over my shoulders.

"Put your arm around my waist and lean," I said.

She did, then she tried to hop, but she stumbled. I quickly put both arms around her to keep her from falling.

"We're not very good at this," she said.

"Nobody is. That's why they invented crutches. Try again."

We gimped together three awkward steps and Bethany stopped. "I'm afraid I'll have to put weight on it and the stitches will rip open."

"There's only one thing to do," I said. Before she could say another word, I bent over and picked her up. She was a little heavier than I thought, but it was a good weight, warm and soft.

"You're going to kill yourself!" she squealed.

"I'm Tyler, the Amazing Hulk. Which way, Your Highness?"

She pointed towards the stairs. "Up."

I got stronger with every step, heart pumping steady. This was better than any fantasy I'd ever had. Her body was muscle-hard, and her skin felt like silk.

"I am your servant, madam," I said. "I vow to carry you everywhere and feed you cake."

"Keep feeding me cake and you won't be able to carry me."

I paused at the top of the stairs. "I'll always be able to carry you."

She blinked.

And then the door to the garage slammed open.

Bethany's entire body tightened. "Chip! What are you doing home?"

Chip froze in the doorway, trying to make sense of the sight of me a) in his house, and b) carrying his sister, who c) was enjoying a) and b).

"What the hell are you doing?" he snarled.

"He's helping me," Bethany said, "which is more than I can say for you. Put me down, Tyler."

Your wish is my command. I carefully lowered her to the ground and helped her sit in a kitchen chair.

Chip pulled out a quart of Gatorade from the oversized refrigerator. He took a few gulps and wiped his mouth on his arm. "Mom wants you down to Monaghan's. She made me come get you."

"Why?"

The cat came out from under the table and twisted itself around Chip's ankles. "They have a bunch of crutches. I'm supposed to drive you over there so you can pick. Dipwad here is not invited."

"I have to go home anyway," I said.

"Are you sure?" Bethany asked. "You could come with us if you want."

Chip put the bottle on the counter and walked back to the door. "Don't be such a slut, Beth. Tyler is leaving." He smirked and made a sweeping motion with his arm, ushering me outside.

I cross the kitchen in two steps. I put my hand around his throat and lift him off the ground with one arm. I heave him across the room. He slides the length of the counter and lands on the kitchen table. The fruit bowl crashes on his head, and an apple lands in his mouth. Little stars dance in a circle over him and his eyes roll up and. . .

"Are you OK, Tyler?" Bethany asked.

"Yeah, um," I said. "I better go."

Chip stepped aside as I crossed the threshold.

Bethany said, "See you tomorrow."

"Huh?" I stopped.

"School's starting, duh? Maybe you can carry me to class."

Chip slammed the door in my face.

I walked through the five-car garage, out the open door, past Chip's Jeep, down the driveway, along the sidewalks of the movie-set neighbourhood of the Hampton Club and Estates.

"See you tomorrow," she said.

The lawn sprinkler of the house on the corner was still flinging water. I stood in the cold spray until I was soaked through to my boxers.

14.

My plan for the first day of school was to roll out of bed, roll into my clothes, roll down the stairs, and roll out the door to the bus stop. One day riding the bus wasn't going to kill me. I had promised Hannah.

She started pounding on my door a full thirteen minutes before my alarm went off.

"Tyler John Miller! You get out of that bed right now! Mom said!"

It sounded like she was going to punch through the door. All those middle-school girl-power sports had made my little sister a lot stronger than she looked.

"Get up!" *Thumpwhumpthumpwhump.* "Mom said! I don't want to miss the bus."

It was going to take a week for her to figure out that high school was school, plus seven levels of social hell (especially for freshman girls), with too much homework and rules dreamed up by psychopaths.

Then we'd see who was eager to get out the door.

*

I pulled on a shirt, boxers, and shorts – all clean in honour of the first day – and trudged downstairs hoping Mom had remembered to go to the store.

Hannah took one look at me and let out a bloodcurdling scream. "You can't go to school like that!"

"Morning to you, too. Any milk, Mom?"

Mom shook a nearly empty milk jug. "You might get half a bowl. I'll go to the grocery store after work, I promise."

Hannah grabbed my wrist in a death grip. "No food until you change. You are not going to school like that."

I wanted to blow her off, but she was halfway to a meltdown. I let her drag me back upstairs, where she handed me a brand-new shirt and shorts and shoved me into the bathroom to change.

Hannah opened the door as I was zipping up the shorts.

"Do you mind?" I asked.

"I don't want to be late." She sat on the edge of the sink. "Turn around. And don't tuck the shirt in. It makes you look like a dork."

"You think?"

"You're going to be late!" Mom called from downstairs.

I untucked the shirt. Hannah tugged at the shorts so they rode lower on my hips.

"Better," she said. She rolled up the sleeves a little to show off my guns. "Much better. Now one more thing." She grabbed a tube of something from the sink and made me bend over so she could rub gunk in my hair. When she was done, she stepped back.

"Take a look," she said.

The mirror showed some guy – a not-too-shabby guy – I'd never seen before: tall, tan, beefy biceps, the hair thing going on, and maybe a little danger in the eyes. I squinted to look even more dangerous, but it made me look nearsighted.

"See? You are officially an asset." Hannah stood on her tiptoes and pecked me on the cheek. "Thanks, Ty. Now hurry up or I'll miss everything."

15.

The bus let us out in front of the building. Hannah was about to burst with excitement, which would have been disgusting because she would have sprayed blood, guts, and glitter in every direction. She was an innocent, a freshman, one of the sad believers who thought high school was where they would be popular and smart and happy – above all, happy.

My sister had watched too many movies.

The enlightened ones – the wounded sophomores, jaded juniors, and wise seniors – we trudged to the door, a prison gang so beaten down we didn't need ankle shackles.

A pearl-white Jaguar XK8 convertible was parked in the

primo visitor's spot at the front. Bethany Milbury and her mom were parked inside it, arguing like cats in a bag.

Knock on the window. Offer to carry Bethany inside. Offer to wash the car with your tongue.

Mrs Milbury was screaming and waving her long, bony mom-finger back and forth in front of her daughter's face. Bethany crossed her arms over her chest and slumped against the seat.

Maybe later.

We trudged some more. As we got closer to the front door, Hannah poked me.

"You OK?" I asked.

"Why are people staring at us?"

They weren't staring, exactly. They were ... watching. All the social radar systems were on alert.

Hannah faked a little smile to a total stranger. "It's you, isn't it?"

She was right, of course. People had ignored me when I was Nerd Boy, but that changed after I was arrested. A third of my fellow students kept their distance, like I might be wearing a bomb strapped to my waist. Another third looked down their noses at me because I had to work with the (*gasp*) custodial staff. The third third was all thumbs-up and "Yo, Tyler!" because spray-painting a couple thousand dollars worth of damage to the school and getting my very own probation officer made me their hero.

A lot of kids would tell you that being taken away in a squad car was the coolest thing I had ever done.

"You're hallucinating," I told my sister.

Mr Hughes stood in the middle of the lobby with a bullhorn in one hand and a walkie-talkie in the other. He stopped mid-bellow to give me the evil eye.

"Mr Miller," he growled.

"Mr Hughes," I tried to growl back.

He tapped the corner of his eye with a finger. "Remember," he warned.

I was supposed to remember the little talk we'd had in his office a couple weeks earlier. Except it wasn't so little. Hughes lectured me so long about consequences and responsibilities that my butt fell asleep.

I was supposed to remember that this was a privilege: I was back in school because so many people – my parents, my probation officer, a couple teachers – had gone out on a limb for me.

I was supposed to remember that I was on thin ice.

I was supposed to remember that I was on a short leash.

(Quite a vision, all those folks standing on a quivering tree branch, with me at the end in a dog collar, skating on a thin layer of frozen pond.)

While he lectured, I had shifted back and forth from one butt cheek to the other, trying to get the blood flow back.

Mr Hughes had pointed out that I wasn't listening. My father agreed with him, nodding energetically. Dad's head bounced up and down so much during the one-hour little talk I thought for sure he'd get a concussion. After we left Hughes's office, Dad yelled at me for being disrespectful. Then he made me remow the lawn.

Mr Hughes stopped tapping the corner of his eye. "Have a good day," he said.

I was overcome by the urge to do something profoundly stupid, like pee on the flagpole or throw myself under a bus, just to see the look on his face.

But my little sister, wide-eyed and fourteen, tugged at my elbow.

"That was the principal, right?" she asked as soon as we were out of earshot.

"The one and only," I sighed.

She dragged me out of the flow of traffic and into an alcove. "Here, hold these." She handed me her books and purse, and rolled up the bottom of her shirt, exposing a new belly-button piercing that looked infected.

"When did you get that?" I asked. "Mom will kill you."

"What she doesn't know won't hurt her." She folded down the top of her miniskirt, showing way too much skin. "I never realized that you had a reputation, Ty. I am so proud of you."

"It's not a good reputation," I pointed out.

"Are you kidding me? The principal hates you. That rocks. How do I look?"

"Like a mistake."

"Shut up." She took her books back and tucked her arm through mine. "It's the attitude, Tyler, all about the attitude. If you act like 'Tyler Miller, emo nerd who is always screwing up,' your life – and mine – is going to suck. You have to be Tyler, the Danger Guy. Gangsta Miller."

"They don't let gangstas on the debate team," I pointed out.

"They should. They might win for a change."

She turned her smile back on, and we rejoined the crowd streaming towards the cafeteria, the worst place in the world for a freshman girl. Which was, of course, why she wanted to go there. A pack of dogs was prowling at the doors, senior guys looking for virgin or semi-virgin freshmen to devour.

"Fix your shirt," I said through my teeth.

"Get over yourself," she said. "I've been waiting my whole life for this."

School was back in session. Let the mind control begin.

16.

Homeroom sucked, because Bethany wasn't there. I figured she was still fighting with her mom.

On the bright side, Chip wasn't there, either.

I had forgotten to look for my schedule before we left the house, so as soon as the Pledge was over, I asked Mr Irwin if he had an extra copy. He rolled his eyes, but he had been a homeroom teacher for one hundred and twenty years, so he was prepared.

He pulled a piece of paper from a pile on his desk. "Here you go, Miller," he said. "Enjoy."

I looked at it once.

Twice. My head hurt.

CRUEL AND UNUSUAL PUNISHMENT
(AKA MY SCHEDULE)

Calculus
Gym
AP English
Lunch
French IV
Study Hall
AP Art History
AP US Government & Politics

Yes, I had agreed to this. But in my defense, we put my schedule together after my first week working at Pirelli's and the blisters on my hands had all popped open and I was so tired I couldn't remember my name. Mom and Dad were both happy with the schedule. I do remember that part. Signing me up for indentured servitude made their eyes sparkle.

It seemed like such a good idea at the time.

So calc baffled me within ten minutes. First period = waste.

In gym, they lectured us about not leaving valuables in the locker room and lectured us about personal safety and lectured us about proper footwear and lectured us and lectured us and lectured us...

After class, I plowed my way down the hall, feeling the eyes, trying to play Hannah's game of Hey, I Don't Give a Rat's Ass About Any of This, and You Should Be a Little Afraid of Me, Just to Be Safe. It was harder than it sounded, walking like a tough guy and keeping my arms flexed and pretending this was natural.

I tripped over a lot of freshmen.

And then I walked into my AP English class.

Oh, the humanity.

On the board, Mr Salvatore had listed the books and the play I was supposed to have read over the summer. I looked around at my classmates, who had, of course, done the readings, highlighted their favourite lines, and written essays about characters and motivation. For fun.

I picked up one of the books and flipped through it. Don't get me wrong, I like reading. But some books should come with warning labels: *Caution: contains characters and plots guaranteed to induce sleepiness. Do not attempt to drive or operate heavy machinery after ingesting more than one chapter. Has been known to cause blindness, seizures, and a terminal loathing of literature. Should only be taken under the supervision of a highly trained English teacher. Preferably one who grades on the curve.*

I talked to Mr Salvatore after class and explained a few things about my summer. He gave me a week to catch up, in light of my special circumstances, then nodded seriously and said it was time for me to "buckle down."

I almost asked him if I was on thin ice yet, but I didn't want to be put on the short leash the first day.

French was kind of a blur – fifty ways to ask for a stick of bread. My study hall was filled with sophomores who reeked of lip gloss and body wash. Art history, well, at least we'd get to look at breasts.

AP US gov & pol was a different story. The teacher went into gory detail about battlefield conditions during the Revolutionary War and explained the best way to kill an opponent with a bayonet. It was cool right up to the moment when he assigned an essay (using three primary sources) due the next day.

On the bus home, I borrowed Hannah's calculator. I had a minimum of six hours of homework, and it was only the first day of class. Six hours of homework a day × 180 days until finals = way too much work.

Welcome to senior year. Bam—face through windshield.

I didn't have a choice. I would have to face the dragon.

I'd do it after dinner, when he was bloated on double pepperoni with onions.

17.

Dad liked to call his lair "the study," but it was just a basement, with spiders and damp patches on the ceiling tiles. His office stuff – desk, computer, file drawers, and bookshelves – filled one corner. A burgundy leather recliner was positioned next to the high-end Bose stereo. His model-train set stretched on a long, custom table in the middle of the room. Framed accounting certificates hung on the walls.

He had retreated down there after dinner. I gave him half an hour, then followed.

He was hunched over his desk, face in the computer screen, wearing a faded maroon University of Chicago sweatshirt and the best headphones money could buy. In the bluish light, it looked like his eyes had disappeared into their sockets.

"Dad," I said.

He didn't move.

"Dad?"

The headphones were plugged into the stereo. A CD case

was sitting on top of it. Wagner. Wagner was a headbanger composer of the 1800s.

I tapped his shoulder. "Dad!"

He gasped and spun around in the chair. Papers scattered on the floor. As soon as he saw it was me, he glared. He pulled off the headphones and dropped them around his neck. The opera voices coming through them were loud, but tinny.

"I knocked," I said.

"I didn't hear you." He bent down to pick up the fallen papers. "Do you need something?"

"I, um." *Deep breath, deep breath.* "Mom says there's more pizza."

He tapped the papers on the desk to straighten them. "Tell your mother I had enough to eat."

"OK."

"Anything else? I have to finish this report."

The air-conditioning kicked in and blew cold, clammy air through the basement. Dad's nose wrinkled. He flung the headphones on the desk, strode across the room, and shouted up the stairs. "Linda? Turn off the damn air-conditioning! It's only seventy-five outside!"

There was something in his voice that made me want to ram his head into the concrete foundation.

"You don't have to say it like that," I said.

"Like what?"

"Like Mom's an idiot. I asked her to turn it on," I lied. "I was hot."

"So why don't you go up and turn it off?"

"So I will, in a minute." I walked over to the model-train layout. He'd spent years building it. Santa drove the engine. The freight cars were loaded down with elves and presents. The track wound through a village, by a lake, and into a mountain tunnel. The mountain was covered by fake snow. Mom's touch.

I rocked the engine back and forth on the track.

"Don't touch that," he said. "You know how fragile it is. Was there something else?"

I wiped my hands on the front of my shorts. "Yeah, um . . . I need to change my schedule."

"At school? Why? Is there a conflict?"

"Three APs plus calc is insane. I'm not that smart, Dad."

"Your grades from last year were good enough to get you in."

"Just barely and only because you and Mom made a big stink about it. I'm not asking to drop all of them – just one of the APs, or let me switch out of calc."

"No. You're not changing anything." He sat down and leaned towards the screen. "I have work to do."

That was Dad code for "go away." I was supposed to say, "OK," and trudge upstairs, grateful he hadn't yelled at me.

But desperate times call for desperate measures. I stepped closer. "I can't do that level of work, sir. Not in every class. I'll flunk."

The muscles tightened along his jaw and up the side of his skull. He inhaled deeply through his nose and rolled his neck from side to side.

"You want me to take care of your problems again." His voice was low.

"You guys forced me into these classes. I'm just telling you it's not going to work."

"When are you going to grow up, Tyler?"

One punch, a long slo-mo shot to the soft underbelly of the beast to make him double over, just one punch, my fist so far inside him that the knuckles scrape on his spine. . .

I tried not to clench my fists.

"I'm so sick of this," he continued. "You expect me to wave a magic wand and make everything all better. Dad will talk to the teacher. Dad will pay for the lawyer. Daddy fix." He spat the words out.

Step closer, two steps, get in his face and remind him that I have him by six inches and probably forty pounds. Pick up the monitor and bring it down on his head, shove the keyboard down his mouth, cram his skinny butt into the trash can. . .

He wiped his mouth with the back of his hand and rolled his neck again. "This discussion is over." He rolled his chair closer to the desk. "You're staying in your classes. And you will quit working for that Pierogi fellow."

"Pirelli. Mr Pirelli. I like working for him."

He looked over his shoulder. "This is not about what you like."

The air-conditioner shut down and the room fell silent, sour air suspended between us.

"I'll be eighteen in November," I reminded him.

He put the headphones on and turned up the volume.

18.

Mom started with the excuses as I came up the steps.

"—he's under pressure at work
—he's depressed again
—he's not good at communicating
—he's worried about money
—he's your father
—you have to give him a chance. . ."

She was still at it when I closed my bedroom door.

19.

Back in middle school, I had spent a lot of time hiding in the library. The guys who were hunting me down never thought to look there.

One day—I can't remember if it was sixth grade or seventh—the library TV was tuned to CNN, and the

BREAKING NEWS banner was flashing in red. The camera zoomed in on a small plane, the kind with two seats and propellers. It had flown into an office tower in downtown Tampa. Twenty stories off the ground. *Smack*. Nothing exploded, nobody in the building was hurt, but a massive steel-and-glass wall had the tail end of an airplane sticking out of it. It took a long time before the reporters would admit it, but the teenager flying the plane was dead on impact. DOI.

I watched the replays obsessively, trying to figure what the kid's last second felt like. Did he feel anything? Did he feel everything? Which would be worse?

I called Mr Pirelli that night and told him I couldn't work anymore because my dad wanted me to concentrate on school. He said he understood. I told him that I wished I did. I reminded him to fill out the paperwork for my probation officer. He said no problem and if I ever needed a job, I just had to ask.

Before I went to school the next day, I stole the Wagner CD and broke it into twelve million pieces with a hammer on the garage floor. I swept the pieces into a plastic bag and tossed it in the neighbours' garbage can.

20.

Bethany Milbury smiled at me in homeroom every day for the next two weeks. The first couple times she did it, I turned around to see who was standing behind me. Then came the day she got up from her seat and hobbled over to sit in the chair in front of me.

"Hi," she said.

(Stunned silence on my part.)

She blinked her eyes. "Are you mad at me or something?"

I choked out an answer and she smiled so brightly that small holes were burned in my retinas. She let me sign her crutch in an open space close to her left hand. She had a packet of Sharpies in her purse. I chose red.

After that I performed superhuman feats of speed to make it to her fourth- and eighth-period classes so I could accidentally be standing close by in case she decided to smile again. She let me carry her books. People were confused— *Why is Beauty with the Dweeb?* I didn't know, either, but as long as she wanted me around, I was going to be there.

Meanwhile, my grades were being sucked into quicksand. I learned that I remembered nothing from Trig, that *Paradise Lost* was not the book they based the survival reality shows on, and that using search-engine translations is a bad way to do French homework.

Luckily, Dad had to work fourteen hours a day because of some government audit. He left a letter taped to my bedroom door, explaining that I should cut my hair if I wanted people to take me seriously.

If my luck held, he'd have a heart attack before report cards came out.

Yoda's campaign to make Hannah fall in love with him was in full swing. He drove her everywhere, even to buy tampons. If she had a test, he helped her study. If she sneezed, he appeared out of nowhere with a tissue. Every time she had a game, Yoda was pacing on the sidelines.

But Hannah was holding out. It didn't matter what Yoda did; she refused to move him from friend-who-was-a-boy status up to boyfriend.

It was killing him. He told me the problem was his lack of jock genes. He had a permanent doctor's note from gym because he had been hurt in there so many times. But to capture the heart of my sister, twerp jockess that she was, he was willing to do something athletic.

After a lot of pleading and attempted bribery, the JV football coach finally gave in and offered a two-week trial. Yoda could manage the team if he fit with the team's "chemistry."

I had a bad feeling about this.

21.

The third Tuesday in September was hot and nasty. The windows on Yoda's Gremlin were all rolled down, and it felt like the plastic seats were melting. As soon as we pulled out of the driveway, Hannah peeled off the shirt Mom made her wear and revealed a scrap of fabric that was just barely keeping her boobs under control. Yoda drove up on the curb and almost clipped a mailbox.

Sisters should not have boobs.

Or mouths. Hannah spent the whole ride yapping about how evil our parents were because they wouldn't let her dress the way she wanted or pierce anything interesting or follow her favourite band around the world.

"Do you think that Dad is being a bigger jerk than normal?" I asked.

"How can you tell?" she answered.

"No, really," I said.

She took a little mirror out of her purse and looked at it while she put on lip gloss. "Mom figures another four hundred years of weekly therapy sessions and he might be able to feel something. Plus his job sucks. Mom said he might get fired."

"Why?"

"No idea."

She ran her tongue over her lips, and Yoda hit the curb again. I yelled at him to stop staring in the rearview mirror.

My sister had to find a different ride to school or we were all going to wind up dead.

22.

Hannah wasn't the only semi-nude girl in school. It was like they had voted for a "clothing optional" day. They weren't completely naked, but they were showing so much skin that you did not have to use your imagination. All over school, guys were walking into walls and open lockers, losing concentration mid-sentence, and having to stop at fountains to drink a gallon of water while waiting for their boners to calm down.

As I stumbled from the front door to homeroom, I decided that these were the most poetic words in the English language: *camisole, strapless, halter, low-rise, thong, belly shirt, peek-a-boo cut-out*, and *spandex*.

It was awesome.

Except that the girls kept getting pissed. An almost-naked hottie would strut down the hall, butt swaying side to side, top of her underwear peeking out of her shorts, hair flowing down her back, jewelry in her belly button, boobs spilling out of her top, big smile, and what would happen? Every guy she'd walk by would say something crude. Or whistle. Or pant or moan or follow her. And she'd get pissed.

Well, duh.

Before the first bell of the day rang, most guys were semi-conscious with lust and most girls were ready to slap someone.

Mornings like that could almost make you love school.

23.

Bethany was AWOL from homeroom. Chip wasn't, but no way was I going to ask him where his sister was. He was deep into his physics textbook, flipping back and forth between it and a handful of note cards. The rumour was that Mr Milbury never let him bring home any grade lower than a 95. If true, that would explain a lot.

I took the longest way I could between my morning classes but didn't see Bethany anywhere. She probably heard about the clothing-optional vote and decided to stay home. She was classy like that.

Damn.

Calc was incomprehensible. I could understand irrational girls and irrational parents. But irrational numbers? Numbers usually made sense, even the imaginary ones. I kept reading the page in my math book over and over again. The only thing that felt irrational was my brain.

In gym, we learned that stretching was important. And that, again, for the record, the school was not responsible for any items stolen from lockers.

Mr Salvatore handed back my compare/contrast essay about God and Satan. It had a zero on it, and "See Me" written in red pen and underlined. It turned out he was serious about the summer-reading stuff. I had forty-eight hours to read *Paradise Lost* and write an essay that proved I read it.

"Don't waste your money buying a piece of garbage from an online essay factory," Salvatore warned me. "I can smell that junk a mile away. And do not waste my time with a first draft. There is power in revision. It's about time you learned that. Oh, and have you heard about this little thing called 'spell check'? You should try it."

24

Must. Eat. Food.

The lunchroom smelled like deep-fried fat and sounded like a packed football stadium. I bought as much food as I could for $2.50 and sat near the door.

Must. Not. Think.

My sister threw herself into the seat across from me. "Do you think Calvin is hot?"

"I'm failing senior year, Hannah."

"And I care? Seriously, do you think Calvin is hot?"

"He's not my type."

"Two of my friends think he's hot because he has a car. Can I have a bite of your cookie?" She took the cookie before I could protect it. "I need five dollars, too, because I lost a bet to Mandy Simpson."

"What was the bet?"

"Whoever got asked out on a real date first. Some soccer player hit on her when she was at her locker. She's such a whore. She'll probably do the whole team by Christmas." She opened her lunch bag. "God, that means I can't go out with any of them."

"Technically, you won."

"What?"

"Yoda – Calvin – has wanted to ask you out for weeks."

"He has?" She munched on a carrot stick. "Well, why doesn't he just ask, then?"

"He's afraid you'll say no. It doesn't matter. I don't want you going out with him or anyone else."

"Why not?"

"Because you're my sister, you twit. Sisters aren't supposed to date."

She rolled her eyes. "Could you be any more ignorant? Tell Calvin I'll say yes. He's sweet and he has a car. What is he, seventeen? Mandy's soccer player is only fifteen. Ha, I win."

I consumed my cheeseburgers in three bites each. Hannah nibbled her rabbit food and drank her water and my chocolate milk and yakked about guys and hot teachers and her new best friends and the need to go shopping. Her words came out as fast as fully automatic machine-gun rounds. She was making my ears bleed.

I was still in shock because I had two days to read a five-hundred-page poem. I pulled Hannah's lunch bag closer and munched some celery.

The door to the cafeteria opened. The lunch monitors scowled. I watched, chewing on the celery cud, while Hannah's mouth flapped. The plastic knob of a crutch poked around the half-opened door. Bethany Milbury hobbled in.

I stared. Why was she here? Bethany never ate lunch with the humans. She went out to lunch with Michelle and Alison from the tennis team, or one of the boys who drove brand-new German sports cars. Why was she here?

She took a few wobbly steps. Even after a couple weeks, she still hadn't gotten the hang of crutches.

I leap over the table just as she slips on the grease-slicked floor. She falls into my arms and whispers, "Thank you, Tyler." As I carry her to the lunch line so she can buy yogurt (for her) and fries and cheeseburgers (for her hero, me), everybody in the cafeteria stands and applauds. The lunch ladies are so moved they give us free cookies.

"Hey, Bethany!" Hannah shouted. "Over here!"

Bethany made her way to our table. (It was closest to the door, after all.) She smiled at my sister. She leaned the crutches against the table and put her hand on my shoulder. My shoulder.

She gracefully sat. Next to me.

She was wearing jean shorts that were short enough but not too short, a pink T-shirt that said "Princess" in cursive, and a candy necklace that I was desperate to nibble on. From every corner of the cafeteria, people were watching.

"Oh, God, you guys will let me sit here, right?" Bethany asked. "It's so hot I can't stand it. My armpits are blistered, I swear. I can't take another step."

I wanted to say something, anything, but by the time I got over the shock, she was deep in conversation with my sister (who I adored very, very much at that point) about crutches and armpit pain. Besides, the wad of celery in my mouth was the size of a grapefruit.

"I love that shirt on you, Tyler." Bethany lifted her left leg and set her bandaged foot in my lap. "It's hot."

Her foot. My lap.

In front of the entire cafeteria.

A collective gasp came out of the crowd.

I was pretty sure that the rest of my life was going to be a bitter disappointment, but at that moment, I didn't care.

25.

I went to my afternoon classes, but I was having dizzy spells. The touch of Bethany's foot was still burning on my leg.

Principal Hughes interrupted the beginning of seventh period to state again, "for the record," the details of the school dress code. Everything interesting was banned, including bathing-suit tops and T-shirts encouraging the consumption of alcohol, drugs, or promiscuous behaviour. Acceptable clothing included pants that rode above the belly button, shirts that reached down below the waist and had sleeves, and skirts and shorts long enough to contact the knee.

Mrs Harrison, my art history teacher, spent the rest of the class talking about the beauty of the human body and showing a PowerPoint presentation of Botticelli and Rubens paintings. In US gov, Mr Clarke hammered home the notion of self-determination and representation.

*

The buzz caused by nearly naked girls and Bethany Milbury's foot was gone by the end of the day, destroyed by my teachers. I was nut-deep in homework alligators and I needed help. I needed the Jedi Master of George Washington High: Calvin "Gifted and Way Talented" Hodges.

But he was not at his car. I went to field-hockey practice. Not there, either. I checked the parking lot again, then the AV room. No Yoda.

Then I heard it.

Yoda had a very distinct scream.

He was in the locker room.

26.

The lights were off, but I could make out five of them standing in a circle in the second locker bay. They were all skinny, zit-faced sophomores in shorts and shoulder pads. One glanced at me as I walked in, sizing me up.

Crap.

Normally I would have snuck out at that point, pretended I made a mistake, phoned in the assault from the lobby. Yoda would have understood; I'd done it before. He'd done it before.

Except I couldn't. I switched into gamemaster mode: no thought no conscience no heart no consequence no stopping. I was left with three abilities: breathing, swearing, and pounding JV jerks into submission.

"What the hell are you doing?" I barked in my brand-new 350-pound-NFL-linebacker voice.

Five faces looked my way.

"Get lost," said the biggest one, who was smaller than me. His name was Parker. He had been at the Milburys' party.

"Maybe we should go," said a henchman.

I stormed towards them. They all stepped backwards, and their circle broke. In the center of the locker bay was the bench, the bench you put your sneakers on when you're tying them.

Yoda was lying across the bench on his stomach, his wrists tied together with duct tape. His jeans and boxers had been yanked down. His butt cheeks had been taped together, too. He kept his head down.

Breathe. Just keep breathing. And kill the first thing you can get your hands on.

"All right, party's over," I said, with more control than I was feeling.

Parker got in my face. "We're just getting started. And I don't remember inviting you."

"You have two seconds to disappear."

"Get lost, Nerd Boy," spit Parker.

The henchmen stepped back into the circle. One of them smacked Yoda with a wet towel. Yoda grunted in pain, trying to hold the sound in. The jerk with the towel laughed, a high-pitched squeal, like a jackal.

I snapped.

I grabbed the front of Parker's shoulder pads, lifted him off the ground, and slammed him against the lockers. His eyes went wide. The henchmen froze, confused. I pulled him towards me and shoved him into the metal doors again. Parker fumbled, trying to get some leverage so he could hit me. I slammed him harder. I was going to do this over and over and over until I drove a Parker-sized hole through the locker, then the locker beyond that, all the way until I broke through to the outside of the building.

"Hey!" someone yelled, the voice far away. "Put him down."

The air split with light as the door from the playing fields opened and Chip Milbury walked in, helmet in hand.

"What's going on?" he yelled.

I took a deep breath and let go of Parker, who stumbled forward.

"Ask him," I said.

Parker quickly explained that Yoda was bothering them because he "thinks he can be our manager".

I kept my back to the lockers and slid a few steps closer to Yoda. I knelt next to him and quickly unwrapped the tape that tied his wrists. As Yoda pushed himself off the bench, I reached out for his arm. He brushed me off and pulled his jeans up over his butt without removing the tape. He zipped his fly and buckled his belt. His eyes never left the floor.

"And you think this is cool?" Chip asked Parker. "You think it's funny?"

"Yeah," Parker said. "Don't you?"

Chip licked his lips and glanced around quickly. "Yeah." He play-punched Parker's arm. "Stupid, but funny." Then he turned to me. "You got a problem with this?"

"Yeah, I do," I said. "He was offering to help, and these little shits jumped him." My voice was getting louder. "Five on one," I yelled. "Five on one! You're all freaks, know that?"

Chip stepped up to my face. "That's a good one, you calling somebody else a freak."

It occurred to me that the odds were now six on one. And since Yoda was useless in a fight, the one was me.

"Got anything else to say?" Chip asked.

The only sound in the locker room was Yoda breathing hard, trying not to sniff. Out in the hall, a couple of girls giggled, their flip-flops smacking the ground. In the distance, coaches' whistles were blowing. Chip Milbury and his friends were about to give me the beating of my life. I had nothing to lose.

"Chicken," I said.

"What?" He was confused.

"You're a chicken," I said. "A coward."

Chip forced a laugh. "And you're a lot dumber than I thought you were."

More silence. This was where they were supposed to jump me, to hold me down and take turns kicking me. But Chip just chewed the inside of his cheek, and Parker had worked his way to the back of the crowd, rubbing his head where it had made solid contact with the locker.

"Aren't you going to flatten him?" one of the guys finally asked Chip.

Chip hesitated. "This is the wrong place," he said.

I had him. Chip was afraid to take me on because there was a chance that he'd lose in front of all his boys. He hadn't forgotten who actually won the arm-wrestling match.

"*Braaaaawck*," I said.

"Hit him," Parker said.

Chip's eyes darted around the room. He wanted to piss his pants. I could smell it. I had won. I had levelled up. I was a freaking giant killer, and they all knew it.

"He's not going to hit me." I was growing taller and stronger by the second. "I'll hit back harder, won't I, Parker?"

Two of the JVs drifted to the door and looked outside.

Chip kept one eye on them and the other on me. "I'm not going to hit you because we're in school and I'm not stupid enough to do anything here," he said.

"Not even if I ask nicely? Not even if I say pretty please?"

Yeah, that was taunting, but I was desperate for Chip to take a swing at me so I could unleash a decade of rage on his ass.

Chip turned to his dwarves. "Get back on the field." As they trooped outside, he pointed at me with his helmet. "Watch yourself, Miller."

"Any time you want, Chipper," I said. "Any place."

27

As we drove home, I kept flashing back to the locker room
and replaying the scene obsessively. Me opening the door.
Me taking control. Me flattening Parker. Me challenging
Chip.

What was I thinking?

They could have killed me. They could have killed us both.
Temporary insanity was the only explanation.

Yoda didn't want to talk about it. He kept his eyes nailed
to the road in front of the car the whole ride. When we got to
the driveway, I did not help him out of his seat. He would have
tried to punch me if I did, then he would have missed, then he
would have felt like an even bigger loser. But I carried his
backpack and I followed him into his house, just in case he
needed something.

"How are you going to get it off?" I asked. (Yoda was a
hairy guy, if you get my drift.)

His bangs fell in his face. "Just leave me alone, OK? Go
home."

I was halfway to the front door when he called, "Wait!"

I stopped. "What?"

"Don't tell Hannah."

"'Course not."

"Thanks. You want a soda?"

I walked back down the hall to his kitchen. We armed
ourselves with food and retreated to the basement to do

something mind-numbing. Yoda wanted to watch *Star Wars: Episode III* again. I wanted to watch *Spider-Man*. We compromised and watched the hot blonde on the Weather Channel talk about highs and lows and tropical storms ready to create havoc. We drank black-cherry soda and ate Doritos.

We didn't talk about football or duct tape or sisters or fathers or crime or punishment. We didn't talk about the time in seventh grade I had my face pushed into a toilet or when he used to get chased home from school or when we both used to hand over our lunch money so we wouldn't get beat up or the plans we used to make to get back at the bullies or how weird all of this was because I had picked that Parker kid up off the ground and slammed him into a locker. We didn't talk about what it felt like when they held him down or how hard he fought against crying or how close I came to killing Chip Milbury or if he needed help getting the tape off because we both knew if he asked, I'd do it, and we'd never talk about it again.

We didn't talk about any of it.

Instead we talked about the odds that the weather babe's boobs were real.

When his mother asked if I was staying for dinner, I said no, I had to go home. Yoda said he'd take care of the *Paradise Lost* essay for me. He had read it for fun and loved it.

Before I left I told him it was cool for him to go out with Hannah.

28

I was in the shower that night when I remembered what I wanted to tell Mom. I jumped out, wrapped a towel around my waist, and hustled down the hall.

She was sitting on top of the quilt that covered her bed, laptop in front of her, a pen tucked behind her ear, reading glasses at the end of her nose. The family calendar was next to her, and CNN was on the TV, muted, the tragedies of the day crawling across the bottom of the screen.

She looked up. "Run out of soap?"

"What? No. You know that shirt you got me? The red one? That I wore today?"

She pushed her glasses up into her hair. "You're dripping on the carpet."

"I need more of those shirts. Like, twenty of them."

"You want me to buy you new clothes?"

"Just get me the shirts. Promise. I really need them."

"Um, fine. I'll get the shirts. Want some pants to go with them?"

"Yeah. But only if they're hot. Not Mom hot. Ask some girl at the store. Make sure she's good-looking. Or take Hannah with you."

"Hot."

"Exactly." I turned to go.

"Hang on," she said.

73

"I'm dripping on the carpet," I pointed out.

"Does this have anything to do with Bethany?"

"Bethany who?"

"Nice try. Your sister told me."

I tightened the towel around my waist. "Bethany who?"

She nodded. "OK, we'll pretend you don't like her. One more thing." She picked up the calendar. "Don't forget your meeting with Mr Benson after school tomorrow. And we're scheduled for the Christmas card photo on Friday."

"No way. We're too old for that."

"I got the last slot, five o'clock, with Davis Gunnarson, and he is a genius – an expensive genius – so we will not be late. We'll leave here at quarter after four. Do you know where your sweatshirt is?"

I shivered. She had the air-conditioning cranked again. "The one with the retarded reindeers? It won't fit."

"The plural of 'reindeer' is 'reindeer.' No *s*. You swam in that shirt last year. It'll be fine."

"But. . ."

"You wanted me to go shopping for new clothes? Something that Bethany would like? What was the word you used . . . 'hot'?"

The question hung there. CNN reported on the rise in the stock market, green arrows everywhere.

"OK." I held on to my towel, leaned forward and kissed her cheek. "Quarter after four, Friday. *Reindeer*. Thanks, Mom."

When Yoda picked us up on Wednesday, he was sitting on a large pillow covered in a Jimmy Neutron pillowcase. I didn't say anything. My sister was too distracted to ask any questions.

Yoda stared at Hannah's field-hockey uniform. "You look amazing."

Hannah looked into a little mirror as she drew a line of thick, black grease under each eye. "We have a game this afternoon."

Yoda shifted into drive. "I know. I'll be there."

She capped the tube and tugged at her skirt. "Did you know that this violates the dress code? It's four inches too short."

"You should protest. Hold a rally."

"Tell me about it," she said. "It's hypocritical fascism."

"You don't know what fascism means," I said.

"Fascism is a totalitarian world view that supports the state – or the school – controlling all aspects of personal life," Hannah said. "I learned that yesterday."

"It's just a dress code," I said.

Hannah picked a piece of lint off her skirt. "Principal Hughes should read about how well fascism worked for Mussolini."

Yoda smiled at her in the rearview mirror. "You have them cornered."

"You've lost your mind," I said.

When I walked into homeroom, Chip Milbury acted like I didn't exist. That was a good thing. Bethany did, too. That was bad. But she was busy handing tissues to Stacey Peters, who had just been dumped, so I forgave her.

When the bell rang, I dropped my notebook so the papers would scatter all over. This made me late to class, but it guaranteed that Chip would be in front of me. One-on-one I could handle Chip Milbury no problem. But Chip had an army on his side. I was still the slightly weird kid who only had one friend.

As my calculus teacher yelled at me for being late, I realized that I needed to work out again. My hard-earned landscaping muscles were beginning to melt. I'd start doing push-ups. I'd run. Maybe Bethany would let me pick her up and practise lifting her.

I'd have to phrase that in just the right way so she didn't slap me.

I was called down to the principal's office at the beginning of second period.

Mr Hughes looked terrible. All of the buttons on his phone were blinking red. His walkie-talkie lay on the desk, crackling. When the secretary showed me in, she reminded him that he had a meeting with the superintendent in five minutes.

"We're keeping this short," he told me after she had closed the door. "My spies tell me there was an altercation in the boys' locker room after school yesterday."

Chip had an army. Mr Hughes had a spy network. I needed to beef up my recruitment efforts.

"Were you a part of that altercation?" he continued.

"No," I said, happy to tell the truth. The *altercation* was the attack on Yoda. I was part of the *aftermath*. A technicality, perhaps, but an important one.

"You're sure?"

"Did someone see me there? Did someone file a complaint?"

He stared at me for a full minute. The seconds dragged on the clock behind him like the hands were stuck in tar. "No," he finally admitted. He tapped a piece of paper on his desk. "I am required to report any trouble you get into to your probation officer."

I nodded. "I'm seeing him this afternoon, sir. Should I ask him to call you?"

Another half minute of silence, then, "No. But your grades are not what one would hope for."

How was I supposed to answer that? I kept my eyes on him and focused on blinking regularly, but not too fast, so I wouldn't look like a liar or a cheat.

"You're walking a fine line here, Tyler. You don't have any room for error."

Blink. "Yes, sir. I know that, sir."

"I don't want to hear any more rumours about you. You keep your nose clean."

"I'll try my best, sir." I sniffed and wiped my nose on my sleeve. He didn't notice.

Bethany sat with us at lunch again. She did not put her foot in my lap, but she had the choice between sitting next to Hannah or me, and she sat next to me.

Her arm bumped mine four times.

After lunch I sniffed my sleeve. It smelled like her. I wanted to strip and rub it all over me, but the lunch ladies were already giving me funny looks.

31.

After school, I took the C bus into town to the county courthouse to meet with Mr Benson, my probation officer. He was a big guy, ex-Marine plus sixty pounds, grey in his buzz cut, thick glasses, and a smile that reminded me of a hungry possum.

The waiting room was the size and temperature of a meat locker and was lit by blinding fluorescent lights. There was a bored secretary at one end and a coffeepot that looked like it had last been used in the late 1980s. Old copies of *Highlights* magazine and *Good Housekeeping* were piled on a metal table in the corner.

I sat.

How did I end up with hardcore stuff like a judge, trial, and probation officer? Look up the laws about property damage.

It's a good thing they never found out what I really wanted to do. Spray-painting the school was Plan B.

The Foul Deed: Plan A involved a bomb, an entertaining smoke bomb that would have forced them to close school on a beautiful spring day. It seemed like a surefire way to become a hero.

Then I found myself dreaming about a real bomb. About blowing up the building. But don't get me wrong, I wasn't going to hurt anybody. I planned on using a timer so that at three o'clock in the morning the entire building would explode into small, standardized pieces.

I just wanted to make a statement.

After a week of planning, I started having nightmares about explosions and timers that went bad. All that broken glass was bound to hurt someone. The fire might spread from treetop to treetop until it hit the neighborhoods around the school, then the stores on Grant Boulevard, and then the Buckeye Mall would go up in flames and the police would corner me and there'd be a tense standoff with their weapons drawn, and as I raised my hands over my head, one of them would think I was reaching for a weapon, and they'd blast away.

I'd be the next dead boy on CNN for sure.

By deciding to spray-paint a few harmless slogans, I actually saved hundreds of lives and countless millions in damages. But when they arrested me, I realized that people might not understand if I explained that part. I never told anyone. I thought about it from time to time, but I never told.

The secretary looked up from her nails when Mr Benson's door opened. A woman my mom's age hurried out.

I followed Mr Benson inside and took my chair. He shuffled papers on his desk and smiled his hundreds of big teeth at me. He told me that he'd had a great report from Mr Pirelli and another nice one from Joe, the head custodian at school.

I nodded.

"How are your classes going?"

"Great," I said.

"How's your dad?"

"Why, did he call you?"

"No. It's just that people like your father want to send their kids to summer camp, not to a probation officer. I wanted to make sure things were OK."

"He's fine," I said. "He works a lot."

"Well, give him my best." He scribbled something on a piece of paper. "That's that. Work hard at school, keep your nose clean, and come back in a month."

*

Again with the clean-nose thing. Authority figures had a pathological fear of boogers, that's how I saw it.

32

The explosion hit us as soon as I opened the door at four thirty on Friday afternoon. Good thing I was in front. Hannah didn't have the body mass to absorb that much punishment.

"OhmyGodwherehaveyoubeendon'tyouknowwhattimeitis you'renotdressed!"

Mom was screaming so loudly she set off car alarms three streets over. She was decked out in black velvet pants, pearl earrings, a necklace of jingle bells, a sweatshirt covered with stoned-looking reindeer, and antlers.

Reindeer.

"Uh-oh," Hannah whispered.

There was no nice way to say it: our mom was a Christmas freak.

Everystinkingthing about Christmas was holy. Not just the church stuff; you could understand that. But the rest of it – decorations brought down from the attic as soon as the Thanksgiving dishes were done, carols playing 24/7, candles with the choking stench of "Holiday Cheer," cookies that were not for eating, but for "atmosphere"; it was nauseating.

Worst of all was the stupid family photo that always went

on the front of our Christmas card. Seventeen years' worth of those pictures were lined up with military precision on the walls of the living room. In the first one, I was a month old. I looked like a deformed vegetable swaddled in a Santa suit.

Hannah and I sprinted upstairs to change while Mom stomped around in the kitchen.

"Where is your father?" she yelled again as she slammed down the receiver of the kitchen phone.

If he was smart, on a plane to Tokyo.

I pulled the sweatshirt over my head. "Why don't we just Photoshop him in?"

"Only if we can add a mustache and cross his eyes," Hannah called from the bathroom.

"I can hear you both," Mom yelled up the stairs, "and you are not funny. Do you know how hard it is to get time with Davis Gunnarson?"

I tugged at the bottom of the sweatshirt, but it stayed at the level of my belly button. I looked in the mirror hung on the back of my door. Not cool.

"I'm not wearing this!" I shouted.

"Wear it or die," Mom shouted back.

Hannah pushed my door open, almost smacking me in the face with it. "Let me – oh, snap!" She couldn't say anything after that, because she was writhing on the ground, pointing at me, and laughing so hard she could barely breathe.

*

Fifteen minutes after we walked in the front door, we were breaking the speed limit to get to the photography studio of Mr Davis Gunnarson. Is there anything more embarrassing than being driven around by your mom? Yes, if you're wearing a reindeer sweatshirt that is two sizes too small.

"I left messages for your father on every number I have for him." Mom accelerated to make it through an intersection as the light turned red. "I emailed him directions to Gunnarson's, too."

"Why can't we just use your camera and take the picture in the kitchen?" Hannah asked.

"Or use your studio?" I added.

"No way," Hannah said. "It smells like dog poo."

Mom did most of her pet photography in clients' homes, but she rented a small, climate-controlled garage for people who wanted to pose their pooch in front of a fake backdrop of a Hawaiian beach or the Egyptian pyramids. And no, I am not making that up.

"The studio does not smell like dog poo." Mom's eyes darted left and right as she coasted through a stop sign. "It's perfectly clean. But my equipment isn't good enough. I'd need better lights, the right filters."

I rolled down my window for some air. "You should buy them, then. You take good pictures. Better than this guy, I bet."

"You think?"

"Hell, yeah. It's time to give up the doggies and kitties."

"Don't swear," she said automatically. She hit the turn signal, checked the rearview mirror, and sped past a taxi-cab. "I've thought about it."

"If you don't kill us in the next five minutes, I'll help you find the space."

"That would be nice." Mom made a hard left into a parking lot and hit the brakes. "We're here."

Dad wasn't.

We waited for an hour, but he didn't show.

Mom had a fit, then rescheduled.

If Dad ever explained why he didn't show up or call, I didn't hear about it. When the mail arrived the next day, it had interim notices from all of my teachers. He came out of his lair long enough to ground me until the end of time. Again. He also confiscated the power cord to my computer.

I spent Sunday combing through the real-estate listings and found two properties for Mom to look at. She didn't sign a lease for either one, but she asked me to please work a little harder at bringing my grades up, and bought me a new power cord.

33.

On the last day of September, we had to attend a senior assembly about college. I sat next to Yoda, who slept. He had already filed his applications. Now it was just a matter of seeing who wanted to throw more financial aid at him.

Chip Milbury and his minions were sitting two rows behind us. I stayed alert in case they decided to lob hand grenades. Chip hadn't retaliated yet, and that made things worse.

The speaker said that college deadlines were firm, correct spelling was important, and choosing a college was a serious decision.

After the assembly, I walked with Yoda to Hannah's field-hockey game. Her team had sort of adopted him as a community-service project after he'd quit football. They thought his glasses were cute. Whenever he kissed my sister (horrifying, yes) the team would all say, "Awwwww!" the way girls do when they see puppies, ponies, and baby ducks.

The coach liked his ability to spot weaknesses in the opposing team. They hadn't lost a game since Yoda sat at the end of the bench, stat tracker in hand.

Hannah was playing center forward with astounding brutality. The referees didn't care, and the other team quickly learned it was less painful to stay out of her way. By halftime she had taken four shots and scored twice.

The second half opened with another lightning-fast breakaway by Hannah and Sue-Jen Parks, giving-and-going all the way to their enemy's goal. Sue-Jen caught a stick to her shin just above the pad and crumpled, but the play continued, with Hannah sprinting across the field just as a defender wound up to fire the ball as hard as she could.

She shot a fraction of a second before Hannah's stick made contact. The ball lifted off the field and traveled in a direct line to my sister's face.

Yoda was off the bench before the ref blew the whistle. I was right behind him.

She was only knocked out for a second. She demanded to be put back in the game, even though the ball had snapped the frame of her goggles. The coach ignored her and told us to take her to the trainer's office.

The office was like an emergency room, with a moaning soccer player bleeding from the mouth on one table and a shivering football player whose foot was stuck in a bucket of ice on another. We laid Hannah down on an empty table. I left messages for my parents at their offices and on their cell phones while the trainer, a short woman with red-rimmed glasses, checked out Hannah's head.

When she finished poking and asking questions, she washed her hands.

"Well?" I asked.

"Nothing critical, but she needs to be seen by a doctor."

Hannah tried to sit up. "It's just a little headache. I have to get back."

Yoda gently pushed her down. "Forget it."

The trainer finished drying her hands. "He's right. Your

doctor will order an X-ray of the skull to rule out fractures. He might want an MRI, too, if he suspects bleeding on the brain."

"Her brain is bleeding?" Yoda asked, the color draining from his face.

"Shhh, not so loud," Hannah said.

"I doubt it," the trainer said. "But doctors like to order tests, and it's better to be safe than sorry. So no more field hockey today. Are you eighteen yet, Tyler?"

"In November," I said. "Why?"

She glanced at the clock. "If you were eighteen I could release her to you. We'll keep trying to get ahold of your parents."

To say I was shocked when my father showed up an hour later doesn't come close.

Dad never showed up for emergencies, not ever. Not when I fell off my bike and needed stitches, not when I fell off my skateboard and needed pins in my arm. Not when Hannah had pneumonia so bad that after they saw the X-rays they put her in intensive care and Mom sobbed in the plastic chair and there was nobody to take me home because I was only five.

But it was Dad standing over Hannah, brushing the hair off her forehead and talking to the trainer about what he should do next.

"Where's Mom?" Hannah asked, as confused as I was.

"Her van broke down outside Hamilton," Dad said. "Shhh."

Hannah's good eye found me and asked, *WTF?* I shrugged.

Dad was looking even rougher than usual, like he was in training for a marathon or was on chemotherapy. But he was there and that counted for something. Half a point, maybe.

Then his cell phone rang. He glanced at the number.

"I'll be right back," he told the trainer. "Have to take this call."

He stepped outside and closed the door, but we could hear him when he started yelling.

"Is he talking to Mom?" Hannah whispered.

I listened. "No, somebody named Stuart. It's work."

She closed her eyes.

When he came back in, the trainer gave Dad a piece of paper with instructions on it. We helped Hannah to her feet. She batted our hands away and grumbled.

Hannah rode with Dad to the ER so a doc could check her out, just in case. Yoda wanted to go, too, but Dad gave him the evil eye and said this was a family matter.

I wound up driving Yoda home in his car because he was so freaked out. Exploding Death Stars was one thing; watching your girlfriend get knocked out cold was another.

34.

The concussion turned out to be minor. The only damage was that Hannah's team lost and she had to sit out the next four games. She sat them out on Yoda's lap. He claimed that her black eye was cute. If aliens had crawled out of my sister's forehead and nested in her nose hair, he would have called it cute.

The day after Hannah's accident, Dad had to leave for some mysterious meeting in Omaha or Topeka or God Knows Where. He and Mom had a screaming match in the kitchen before he left. The postal look on his face when he stalked out to the taxi made me think I should steal the gun hidden in his bottom drawer and toss it in the river.

Mom kept busy photographing dogs in Santa hats and antlers for other people's Christmas cards. I helped her by combing the real-estate listings for better studio space. She said it was impossible to find a landlord who wouldn't mind that most of her clients had four legs and unpredictable bathroom needs. I suggested again that she should take pictures of people, who were generally better at using a toilet. That made her laugh.

We didn't talk about Dad or Omaha.

Bethany was able to ditch her crutches a couple days after Hannah got creamed. I was afraid this meant the end of our relationship. Not that it was exactly a relationship, not quite. But she would sit next to me at lunch a couple times a week and she grabbed or punched my arm an average of 1.2 times a day and she waved to me in the halls and she hadn't blocked my screen name, so there was hope. I did push-ups every night until my arms shook.

Chip and I had reached a standoff. He didn't like me talking to Bethany, standing near Bethany, or kissing the ground that Bethany walked on – that much was obvious – but he just stared at me like a gorilla and cracked his knuckles whenever I was around. The knuckle-cracking was supposed to intimidate me. Maybe if I was a walnut or a pecan. And the staring? He had miles to go before he came close to competing with my father.

Dad came home after four days spent in God Knows Where. He didn't say anything when he walked in, just set his suitcase in the laundry room and went straight downstairs.

Two weeks into October, I finally figured out how to get Gormley across the Tophet sulphur pits. All he had to do was to lash himself to a Nightmare. *Duh.* I levelled up (down, actually) to Thirty-Six, the Frozen Plains of Despair. The time I dedicated to crossing the Pit contributed to a failed calc quiz and the plunging of my government grade from a solid C to a whiny D, but you have to make sacrifices if you're going to get anywhere in Hell.

35.

Our homecoming football game had always been held on Friday of Columbus Day weekend to give everyone an extra day to recover from the hangovers.

No, not really.

It was on Friday of Columbus Day weekend because our archrivals, the Forestdale Bulldogs, needed that extra day for hangover recovery. We Washington Warriors prided ourselves on intelligent drinking. That's what people said, anyway.

Since our football team was 0 and 7, there was not much interest in the game itself. There was a lot of talk about parties that I was not invited to, but nobody bothered about our chances.

That all changed when we got to school on Friday.

Instead of the normal crowd hanging in front of the building, streams of chattering people – looking strangely awake – were hurrying towards Warrior Stadium. There the police had cordoned off the gate with yellow crime-scene tape. We ran around behind the bleachers to stare through the chain-link fence.

"Those bastards," my little sister muttered.

Someone, some deviant Forestdale Bulldog, had burned WARIORS SUCK! into our sacred football sod with weed killer.

My fellow students swore vengeance and punched the fence until it jangled. Members of the football team were told to kill the opposition so that we could regain our lost pride. This wasn't just a prank; it was a declaration of war.

I stood very still. Were people staring at me? Did they think this was my handiwork? Did they think I would stoop so low?

Of course they did. I was the moron who specialized in misspelled defacings of school property. Maybe I should curse loudly. Or hawk up a loogie and spit on the ground, just to prove that I was not a traitor.

I twisted my head around, looking for Chip and the Chipettes, half expecting them to drag me on the field, tear me limb from limb, and set my corpse on fire. I didn't do this, did I?

"Hannah, where was I last night?" I whispered.

"What are you talking about, you idiot?"

"Just help me out. What was I doing last night?"

"You tried to pay me to IM Bethany and convince her to go out with you. And then you took a shower that was so long you emptied the hot-water tank."

Oh. That.

"Thank you," I said.

I couldn't have done it. It wasn't me. Good. Sometimes I scared myself, because once you've thought long and hard enough about doing something that is colossally stupid, you feel like you've actually done it, and then you're never quite sure what your limits are.

36.

Principal Hughes went on the loudspeaker during homeroom to assure us all that the police were investigating the crime and that the criminals would be found. No retaliation of any kind would be allowed, but we were supposed to encourage our football team to do their best.

Bethany said something to me right after the announcement, but with all the whooping and hollering and the ringing of the bell, I couldn't hear her.

I leaned closer. "Say that again?" She smelled like cinnamon, and her lips were wet.

She smiled and pushed her hair back. "I said, are you going to the game tonight?"

"What game?"

She laughed as if I had just made a joke and gave my shoulder a little shove. "The football game, duh."

"Um, I could be. Should I be?"

Do not touch her, I warned myself. *Do not touch her, kiss her, bury your face in her hair, or throw her over your shoulder and head for the nearest cave. Those would all be bad choices, and they would have immediate, negative consequences. No touching.*

"Well, yeah, Tyler. That would be nice." She picked up her books and settled them on her hip. "It would be nice if you came to the game. It would be nicer if you sat next to me. And it would be nicest if you brought me a cup of hot chocolate because it's going to be cold tonight. Got to go. We're late."

Don't ask what happened for the next eight hours. I'm pretty sure I was unconscious.

37

Yoda stayed after school to watch Hannah's game. I walked home. It was finally sinking in – Bethany wanted me, *ME!* – to sit next to her. That was extremely close to a date, which was a half step away from permission to make out and touch her glorious private bits and so on and et cetera.

A car almost ran me over a block away from the school. I growled at it and bared my teeth. My testosterone was peaking at world-record levels. I had new hair sprouting on my chest and stomach. I was turning into a wolfman with a life-threatening hard-on, all because a cinnamon-smelling girl wanted me to sit next to her.

I took another shower as soon as I got home. I also took some personal time to think things over. (Not going into details, thank you very much.) Then I set my alarm clock and fell asleep for a couple hours. Being wanted by the woman of your dreams is exhausting work. I slept through the alarm. I had thirty minutes to become confident, manly, shaved, dressed, relaxed, and sitting on a metal bleacher armed with several gallons of hot chocolate.

Crapcrapcrapcrap.

I took another shower, a quick one, because I was already beginning to stink of panic. I cut my chin shaving. I dressed in boxers and socks (all clean), one of my new shirts, a sweatshirt, jeans (clean, too), sneakers, then ran downstairs. Yoda had just arrived. Hannah was all ready to go out.

I was just about to ask Mom if I should make the hot chocolate or buy some at Starbucks when Dad's car pulled in the driveway.

Hannah's eyes widened. "Why is he so early?"

"This is early?" Yoda asked.

"Way early," she said.

I was thinking we should sneak out and run for the hills, but Dad stormed in before I could say anything. We watched him walk into the kitchen and put his briefcase on the table. He took off his jacket and draped it over the back of a chair. He loosened his tie, then stopped, as if he had just noticed the four of us standing there.

"What are you doing home?" I blurted out.

"I live here," he explained. "And it's dinnertime. It's been a while since we sat down together, and—"

"We can't eat dinner," Hannah said. "It's Homecoming tonight. We have to leave or we'll be late."

Dad put his hands up like a traffic cop. "Whoa right there, young lady. Who are you going with?"

Yoda raised his hand like he was in a class. "I'm taking her, Mr Miller."

Dad tilted his head to one side, confused. "Calvin?"

"Yes, Calvin." Hannah grabbed Yoda's hand and started for the door. "I'll be home by eleven."

Dad's voice turned icy. "You do not have permission to leave."

Hannah froze. Yoda swallowed hard.

"I'm going out, too," I said, in an unfortunately high voice. I cleared my throat. "They're going with me. We're all going together. To the game."

"Like hell you are."

"Dad, I have plans," I said, visions of every straight guy in school on their knees offering hot chocolate to the Goddess Bethany.

Mom stepped between us and picked up Dad's jacket. "Look, Bill. I'll cook a nice dinner tomorrow." She folded the jacket neatly over her arm. "Why don't you and I go someplace quiet, catch up with each other?"

"I want dinner. With my family. In my house. Tonight," Dad announced. "End of discussion."

"I'll make some quick sandwiches and heat up some soup," Mom said. "And we have leftover chicken. Extra crispy."

Dad smacked the counter with his hand so hard that the bowl of apples jumped. He waited until the echoes died away before he spoke quietly.

"We have a freezer packed with food," he said. "Please make me a decent dinner." He picked up his briefcase. "Calvin is going home. Hannah can stay in her room until it's time to eat. And Tyler? Mow that goddamn lawn."

I weighed my options.

Was the chance to sit next to Bethany for a couple hours worth the guaranteed wrath of my father, which would include a night of bellowing rage, the total annihilation of my

96

self-esteem, broken dishes, and possibly getting tossed out of the house?

Well, yeah, of course it was.

But it was not worth the nastiness that he would also inflict on my sister, who already had a tear slipping over the faded bruise from her black eye, and my mother, who was pouring herself the first tonic-free gin and tonic she'd had in weeks.

Yoda left.

Hannah slammed her door.

I stayed and mowed the lawn as badly as I could, as the streetlights flickered on, dreaming up one thousand and one ways to hurt the man who spawned me.

38.

Mom did it. She cooked a sit-down dinner for four: pork roast, baked potatoes, steamed carrots, and a side salad with your choice of dressing. Sure, it was nine p.m. by the time we got to eat, but you couldn't rush perfection.

"Pass the pork, please," Dad said.

Mom had decided to pass on dinner. She was passed out on her bed. The cover story was that she had a migraine. What she really had was enough gin to put down a horse, and a desire to shove that roast up Dad's—

But no, honest, her migraines were always the worst when the seasons were changing. It had to do with barometric pressure.

Hannah passed the meat platter to Dad.

"Another piece, Tyler?" Dad asked.

Throw a potato in his face. Smash the platter over his head. Pick up the table, throw it through the sliding-glass door, then heave him out, too. Find a grenade...

"Butter, please," I said.

Hannah passed me the butter.

I divided a half stick between two baked potatoes. Hannah had scooped out the inside of her potato and was mashing it on her plate. Dad cut his slice of pork. The knife squealed on the plate. Dad did not flinch. He cut and chewed, cut and chewed.

"How was school?" he asked.

Hannah spooned cold, overcooked carrots onto the potatoes. "Fascist."

"You don't even know what that means," Dad said. "Heh." (That was supposed to sound like laughter.)

"Yes," Hannah said carefully, "I do. We're studying it."

Dad grunted.

Coming home at a decent hour, forcing Mom to cook, making jokes at the table: something was desperately wrong with my father. I studied him whenever he looked at Hannah. It wasn't the bloodshot eyes, or the stain on his tie, or the twitch in his left cheek. It was what I got when I put those things together.

Ever smell the milk jug when you open it and you don't

think you smell anything funky, so you pour a big glass and you take a giant gulp and as soon as it hits your mouth you know it has gone bad and you spit it in the sink and race upstairs to gargle? And when you finally stop needing to heave, you realize that you did smell something funny at first, but you didn't know what to call it?

That's what I thought of when I looked at my father.

"What else are you studying?" he asked my sister. "How's algebra?"

Hannah obliterated the carrots with the tines of her fork. "Algebra is fine." She blended the carrots and potatoes together. "Not that you care," she added under her breath.

"What did you say?" Dad asked. "Stop playing with your food. Is there a problem?"

Hannah pushed her chair away from the table. She stood up and let her napkin float to the ground.

"May I please be excused?" Her voice shook a little.

"You haven't finished," Dad said.

"I'm not hungry and I still have homework. Algebra homework."

Dad made her stand there a full minute before he answered. "Fine."

Hannah couldn't hold it in any longer. As she bolted from the room, she said, "And I'll check on Mom." She started sobbing halfway up the stairs.

We looked at the empty doorway and listened until a door slammed overhead.

Dad carried his empty glass into the kitchen, dropped a couple ice cubes into it, and unscrewed a bottle. He came back carrying a full glass of scotch, his third. That was weird, too. He never drank more than one a night.

I reached for the pepper. "How's work?"

"Pass that over here, will you?" he asked.

I handed him the shaker. "You've seemed, um, busy."

He shook the pepper on his carrots. "That's one word for it." He put down the shaker, picked up his glass, and took a long, slow sip.

I waited, but he just sat there, elbow leaning on the table, glass in his hand, looking down at the spot where Mom wasn't sitting. He turned the glass so the light from the chandelier caught and reflected off it. "Some of the branch offices aren't playing by the rules." He looked at me over the rim. "Playing by the rules cuts into commissions."

"Why is this your problem?"

"Because I'm Compliance, and the feds are investigating. . ." He took a big slug of scotch and set the glass down heavily. "Enough of that. I've almost got it under control. Your last probation meeting is coming up, isn't it?"

I shook my head. "Two more. One in a couple weeks, one in November."

"I told you it would go fast." He speared a piece of meat and put it in his mouth. "Another couple months and no one will remember it ever happened."

Except the entire student body, police force, and anyone within a fifty-mile radius of my school.

"I'll go with you," he added.

"What? Where?"

He talked while he chewed. "To your probation meeting. The last one. I'll make sure all the loose ends are tied up." He cut the fat off the next bite of meat and pushed it to the edge of the plate. Dad hated the feel of fat in his mouth.

"You don't have to. It'll waste a whole afternoon. Maybe Mom could go."

"Your mother and I have already discussed this. She said she told you."

"I bet it slipped her mind—"

Out of nowhere he smacked the table with his left hand. "Dammit! She promised!" The veins running up the sides of his neck beat like writhing snakes.

"Whoa, hold on – Mom must have forgot. Her migraines. Dad? Are you OK?"

He took a deep breath and blinked. Then he stuck another piece of meat in his mouth. "Of course I am, what a ridiculous question. I was just surprised, that's all."

I looked at my plate so I wouldn't have to watch him chew. "Is there any chance they won't expel my record?"

"*Expunge*. The word is *expunge*. You keep your nose clean and you pull your grades out of the toilet, it will be like it never happened. This pork is tasty, don't you think?"

*

Like it never happened.

Like my mother was lying down because of a migraine.

39

Homecoming Friday Night Play-by-Play Action:

Looked at French book by Albert Somebody = .25
   hours
Printed out English essay Yoda emailed = 2 minutes
AP art history reaction paper = 15 minutes
IM = monitored constantly—the entire world was away
Doodled breasts in government textbook = 20 minutes
Surfed online journals = when I got sick of reading
   away messages
Online porn = you don't want to know
Snack = leftover KFC followed by handful of Tums
Thought about ripping out drywall with my bare
   hands = every other minute
AP calc = .75 hours before I threw the book in the
   trash
Played Tophet = 5 hours

Level Thirty-Six in Tophet looked like Antarctica with the
temperature hovering around seventy degrees below zero. I

was confused. Hell was supposed to be too hot, not too cold. But level Thirty-Six was Inuit Hell.

I had to spend way too much gold on a fur-lined jacket, pants, and boots for Gormley. I sacrificed a spell to start a fire so he wouldn't freeze to death. You couldn't really die in Hell; you'd be reincarnated as a weaker being over and over again until you were reduced to a wormspirit.

My father's Hell level had not shown up yet. Maybe it was being trapped in a office with a screaming boss whose butt you had to kiss day and night. Maybe it was coming home to a wife and kids who bolted for the door when they saw you. Or it was waking up every morning knowing you had to do the same exact thing you did the day before and the day before, like that guy who had to roll the boulder up the mountain over and over, except you'd know that when you died there'd be no relief, because you were already dead and this was what you won as the booby prize in the game of Eternal Soul Roulette.

I wondered what the devil would say to my father. Would they watch baseball? Discuss the bond market?

I fell asleep with my head on my desk.

Dad woke me up at five a.m. He was already dressed for work: black suit, white shirt, gray tie. He said he had to get to the office early.

I did not tell him it was Saturday. I wasn't in the mood for a confrontation.

40

On Monday morning my father went to his office again.

My mother ate dry toast for breakfast, then she went to work, too. She had to take pictures of the mayor's terriers wearing red-and-green plaid vests.

My sister and I went to school. We learned that we had lost the homecoming game.

The perfect American family continued to lead their perfect bullshit lives perfectly.

In order to convince Bethany that I was not a rude, disgusting pig, I spent homeroom apologizing one hundred thousand times for standing her up at the game.

"It's OK," she said again. "Honest. I get it. You've seen my mother. I understand parents who freak out, trust me. Is that a new shirt?"

"Yeah, I guess," I said, praying that I had taken off all the tags. "My mom bought it."

"I like it, but you know what, Tyler Miller?" She focused her eyes on me. The rest of the world was sucked away into a giant vortex, leaving only the two of us. "You are too old to let your mommy buy your clothes."

"I am? I mean, yeah, I am."

"You should go shopping with me. I'll take care of you."

Oh, dear God, will you ever. I was experiencing a noticeable lack of penis control. I slouched a little in my seat to hide the bulging evidence.

She didn't notice. She turned around to ask Mikhail Roberts, sitting behind her, if he did the chem homework. But she did not offer to take him shopping. *Ha.*

42.

Bethany flirted with me for the next two weeks. She also flirted with a soccer halfback named Stefan; Evan, who had the drum solo in the marching band; both of the Prakesh brothers; and Parker, the moronic sophomore who I put through the gym locker. I figured the only thing she saw in Parker was the Corvette he had been promised for his sixteenth birthday. Bethany was smart like that, always looking ahead.

If you lined me up with the other guys, you'd start singing "One of These Things Is Not Like the Others" from *Sesame Street*. The other guys, they all blurred into each other: rich, smart, athletic, and popular. Me, I stood out, the semi-bad boy guaranteed to bring some spice into her life.

Of course, there was always the chance that she was totally setting me up for major humiliation or that this was all mercy-flirting. But, honestly? I didn't care.

*

You could tell that Halloween was just around the corner when the Christmas decorations went up at the mall. The weather finally turned cold, and girls started wearing turtlenecks that showed their belly buttons.

Bethany owned a black cashmere turtleneck. It was a little longer than the other girls' but short enough to flash a quick hint of belly skin when she reached up to fix her hair. She was now touching me an average of 2.4 times a day.

The day the doctor gave her permission to play tennis again was the first day she hugged me. Hug #1. She hugged a bunch of other people, too, including all her girlfriends on the team, Zithead Parker, and both Prakesh brothers, but she was enthusiastic like that.

When I saw Mr Benson at the courthouse that afternoon, he said I looked different.

"Got a girl?" he asked.

"Nah." I shook my head.

"Nothing like a woman to lift a man's spirits. Be safe. See you next month."

The night of the first hug, I dreamed about beating Chip Milbury into a bloody pulp. He got in a couple of good shots; I lost a tooth and my mouth was bleeding. My last punch sent him flying off the roof we were standing on. We were so high in the air, I didn't hear him land.

And then Bethany was in my arms, and she wasn't mad at

all that I had just obliterated her brother. I put my fingertips under her chin.

My heart beat so fast I thought I was going to die.

I moved in slowly . . . and kissed her pink cupcake mouth.

She kissed back. Harder.

I was thinking raw caveman thoughts, but this time it wasn't about beating a guy to death. I wanted a woman, I wanted this woman.

I cradled the back of her head in my hand. A strand of her hair fell into my eyes. The universe was spinning, and this kiss was the only thing that mattered. Bethany opened her mouth. Her tongue glided over my broken teeth. We tasted like blood and frosting.

And I woke up.

The dream was a sign, a magical intervention by all the saints and spirits in charge of helping dweeby guys desperate for a girlfriend.

Those saints and spirits had nothing to do with decent grades, though, which is why the next day began with another calc quiz. But I forgot about it as soon as I was out the door, because she was standing there, waiting for me.

I almost swallowed my tongue.

"Hey, Tyler," she said.

"Hhhn," I answered.

"Thought I'd come see you for a change. So, um, you going to the game tonight? 'Cause I am. And then, well, then I'll be at Rawson's house – Josh Rawson? His parents are in Jamaica. It'll be a great party."

"Hhhn?" I asked.

She blinked her eyes in slow motion. I wracked my brain trying to come up with something intelligent to say, something that would make sense, anything to keep her standing close enough so that I could keep smelling her perfume because it was hitting my brain like crack cocaine.

"Hhhn," is what I finally came up with, for the third time.

"You big dummy," she said with an exaggerated sigh. "I want you" (she put her hand on my left forearm and slid it up under the rolled-up sleeve) "to go with me" (she stepped so close I could feel the heat coming off her body) "to a crazy Halloween party."

I regurgitated my tongue and looked around at the crowded hall. "You're not joking, are you? I mean, you know what I mean. You're not punking me – nobody is filming this or anything?"

"No, silly," she said. "Look, I like you. We're not going out, but I like you, OK? I want to spend time with you. Are you getting the hint here?" Her fingers curled around my bicep.

"Oh, uh, yeah. Ah. . ."

While I struggled to remember a single word of my native language, the bell rang. Bethany pulled away from me. I shivered.

"You don't have to pick me up or anything. I'll be at the

bonfire tonight, and then the game. See you there? If your dad doesn't go off the deep end again, I mean."

"Yeah, um—"

She was already gone, her ponytail bouncing down the hall.

43.

I was so desperate to make this night happen, I took the school bus home. The underclassmen stared at me like I had lost my mind. I nearly told them I had an almost-date with Bethany Milbury (*I'll see you tonight, right?*), but that would have tempted fate, so I scowled at them instead.

I made it to my house at eight minutes to three. I had four hours before the bonfire started. Hannah had a game and Mom was shooting Labradors. Dad was the unpredictable one. I would make a preemptive strike.

The lawn hadn't been mowed since the Night of the Roast Pork Migraine, and it showed. In fact, our entire yard looked trashy. It wasn't just the overgrown grass or the dying marigolds or the scraggly boxwood bushes. It was the gutters where rotting leaves had spilled onto last year's broken Christmas lights, the paint flaking off the shutters, and the mailbox that tilted to the right.

I couldn't fix all of that now. I just had to mow the lawn and sweep the cut grass off the sidewalk. I accomplished both in record time. After I showered I wrote a note to Mom explaining that I was spending the night at Yoda's. I took off before anyone got home.

The Warrior tradition of holding a bonfire before the Halloween football game used to be a big deal. They say you could see the smoke for miles, that kids would party like crazy in the cornfields behind the school, that there were rivers of beer and the occasional sacrifice of virgins. Then the lawyers got involved.

Now the whole thing was closely monitored by the fire department and the police. The bonfire itself was almost big enough to cook a couple hamburgers on. The cornfields had been plowed under and turned into McMansion developments. The Key Club sold cider and fresh doughnuts. The fear of litigation had turned a pagan rite of passage into a pathetic shadow of its former glory.

Some of the kids were wearing Halloween costumes, but most of us had on winter jackets. It felt cold enough to snow. I opened a twelve-pack of spearmint gum. A few teachers mingled in the crowd, friendly-like, standing close enough to students to smell their breath and stare in their eyes. I chewed stick after stick and tossed the silver gum wrappers in the fire. The lights went on in the stadium and the marching band warmed up. The Key Club closed down the cider stand.

Bethany and her friends finally arrived as the bonfire was

dying down, and people were hustling from the parking lot to the stadium so they wouldn't miss the kickoff. The girls were wearing matching Halloween costumes – a cross between an angel and a fairy, with black leggings, tiny skirts made of fabric leaves, low-cut skintight shirts, and wings. A couple girls wore devil's horns in their hair, which spoiled the effect. Not Bethany. Her white-feathered wings fluttered as she walked; her hair caught the breeze and played around her head like magic. She looked like she could fly away to the stars if she wanted.

"Tyler!"

She danced ahead of the other fairy angels and ran up and put her arm through mine. Her eyes sparkled in the firelight and her cheeks were red.

"Ohmigod you wouldn't believe it Stacey's mom's car got a flat tire and we didn't know what to do so then we called Triple-A and Stacey called her stepdad and some guy came out of his house and he had the wheel off before anybody could say anything and then he said we could go in his house, but we were all like, *Whoa, strange guy, I don't think so*, and then the Triple-A guy and the stepdad showed up, and anyway, that's why we're late. God, it's freezing. Did you miss me?"

Somehow my hand slipped behind her head.

Somehow I bent my face down to hers. Somehow her lips opened. Somehow I kissed her and somehow she kissed back.

The bonfire roared and reached for the sky.

44

Apparently we lost the football game. I didn't notice.

Bethany started shivering right after we sat down on the bleachers, so she took off her wings and put on my jacket. I was frozen within minutes, but it didn't matter. I kept her wings on my lap. I counted the freckles and the sparkles on her cheeks. I bought her popcorn and hot chocolate. I did not lick the spot of chocolate off the corner of her mouth. I did not make passionate love to her on the bleachers. Thought about it, but didn't do it.

When I bought the second round of hot chocolate, she confiscated my wallet and went through it, snorting at the picture on my student ID, cooing at the photos of Hannah when she was little, and arching an eyebrow at the patient condom that had lived in there for years.

It wasn't like we were going out. Not exactly, not officially. But we were at the she-gets-to-go-through-my-wallet stage, and I had kissed her – in front of police, armed with guns – and she had kissed back instead of having me arrested.

There was a chance that somehow this was really happening. I didn't know how, but I wasn't going to question anything.

The whistle blew. Game over.

I walked her to Stacey's car, which was jammed full of girls.

In the middle of a crowded parking lot, Bethany kissed me

again. It was a quick kiss but it was a) public, and b) her initiative. Two kisses in one night. I was on a roll. (There was also a chance that I was hospitalized in a deep coma and that this entire night had been a hallucination, but so what?)

Stacey hit the horn.

Bethany handed me my jacket and took her wings back. "I'll see you at the party, right? Sorry we can't give you a ride, but there's no room."

"No problem," I said. "No, wait – problem. Where is it again?"

She rolled her eyes. "Rawson's house? You doof, don't you know?"

"Um, no. How do I get there?"

She grabbed a pen out of her purse and wrote the directions on my palm. She blew on it to dry the ink. My knees buckled. She giggled and gave me a quick kiss good-bye on the cheek.

"Don't be late," she whispered.

45.

OK, so maybe I should have admitted that I didn't have a car, and that my father had confiscated my license when I was arrested for the Foul Deed, and that technically, going to a party like this would be a massive violation of my probation. But that's the kind of thing you have to build up to in a conversation, and there wasn't time for that, not with Stacey blowing the horn and cars squealing out of the parking lot.

I figured it would take me a half hour to get to the party on foot.

Idiot. Moron. Cretin. Fool.

Two hours and a couple of blisters later, I finally made it.

I'd heard of Josh Rawson (who hadn't?) but never had classes with him so I wasn't sure what to expect. Standing on his front porch, it was obvious the place was crowded and noisy, but I didn't know the guy and wasn't exactly invited, not by him, so was I supposed to ring the doorbell, or knock, or sneak in the back?

I rang the doorbell.

Nobody answered.

I reached out to press the button again. The door flew open and I jumped back. Two guys hustled a third guy down the steps as fast as they could. They made it to the driveway before he started ralphing. They yelled at him for splattering their shoes.

I walked in.

"Bacchanalia" summed it up nicely: a party that smelled in equal parts of cologne, beerpuke, peppermints, and weed. Rawson had better pray his parents decided to relocate to Jamaica permanently, because this one was going down in the history books.

The living room was on the right. That's where the

speakers were set up. They had already blown a woofer but kept the volume cranked so that the ragged edge of the sound made the walls shake. Girls were dancing with each other and boys were loving it, dancing behind them and snapping pictures with their camera phones. I saw a couple of the fairy-angel gang, their tiny leaf skirts flirting with being torn off, but no Bethany.

On the other side of the entryway was the dining room jammed with bodies packed around a table overflowing with bags of chips and pretzels, bowls of Halloween candy, and cartons of onion dip that had been used as ashtrays. On the far side were steps that led to a sunken family room that contained mostly horizontal bodies. I hoped she wasn't in there.

The kegs were in the kitchen. Chip Milbury was, too, with Parker and the other nitwits. They were starting to scowl in my direction when Bethany stepped out from behind them.

"Tyler!" she squealed. "Tyler, Tyler, Tiger-Tyler!"

My fairy angel stumbled towards me carrying two red plastic cups sloshing with beer. Her wings were gone and she was wearing a Warriors sweatshirt that reached to her knees and had a wet stain on the front. Her hair was tangled and tucked behind her ears and she was grinning like a kid on Christmas morning.

"You're l-l-late," she slurred.

"I got lost. Having fun?"

"Oh, yeah." She handed me a cup. Her left eye drifted

towards her nose. "Drink," she commanded. "You need to catch up."

I sipped and tried not to shudder. *Cow piss.* I set the cup on the counter.

"Want to go outside?" I asked.

"What?"

"It's noisy!" I shouted.

The crowd around the keg chanted, "Chug! Chug! Chug!" as a guy dressed as a pirate put his mouth on the tap and pulled the handle. I took her hand and motioned for her to follow me.

My plan? What plan? I was winging it.

Parker moved quickly behind the crowd and cut off our exit. He stepped in front of me. "What are you doing with her?" he demanded.

"Out of my way," I said.

He put his hand on my chest.

Oh, crap. Now I have to shove him and he'll have to shove me, and I'll trip and he'll jump on me and people will scream and pour beer on us and I won't get to kiss her.

Bethany grabbed Parker by the thumb and twisted it painfully. "He's with me." She grabbed my hand and dragged me away.

I grinned at Parker and winked.

To be honest, I had never been at a party like this. I mean, I'd been at parties, I had done a little drinking, but this was off the hook and I was off balance. Bethany was totally at home. She wanted to dance, we danced. Well, *she* danced – dirty danced – and everyone watched. I moved nervously from one foot to the other. Part of me wanted to kill all the other guys in the room, part of me wanted to keep them alive so they'd have to deal with the fact that she was dancing with me. Me. Tyler Former Loser Miller.

She wanted to go down to the basement, so down we went. She wanted to play pool, we played. She wanted to watch some kids on the PS2, we watched, with my hand on her hip and her hand in my back pocket. She wanted to drink. I got her another beer, but I didn't get one for myself because out of the corner of my eye I was always seeing Chip and Parker, and they were not happy with the way the night was turning out for me.

When Bethany went to the bathroom with two of her girlfriends, I wandered back to the kitchen in search of real food. Yoda was pouring a cup of foam from the keg with Hannah wrapped around him like a bloodsucking leech.

Yoda was at the party, with my sister.

My sister did not belong there.

She belonged at home, in her bed, alone, asleep, with one arm around her Raggedy Ann and the other under her pillow. My brain and hormones slammed into reverse, and I had to lean against a wall because the room was spinning.

Hannah looked up and pointed at me, her mouth hanging open in horror. "What are you doing here?" she shrieked.

"What are *you* doing here?" I answered.

"Hello? I was invited."

"Liar."

Yoda put his hands up. "OK, you two, that's enough."

"Shut up," Hannah and I both said.

"Take her home," I told Yoda.

"Get over yourself," Hannah said. "You are not going to ruin this for me."

"Um, guys?" Yoda asked. "Can't we just get along? It's a big party."

Hannah chewed her bottom lip. "You don't tell, I won't tell."

"Deal."

"I don't know who you are tonight."

"Fine with me." I leaned closer to Yoda. "Keep her out of trouble."

"Don't worry," Hannah butted in. "We have other things planned."

"I'm going to pretend you did not just say that."

Bethany snuck up behind me, slid her cool hand into mine, and pulled me away. The look on Hannah's face was totally worth it.

We danced to two more songs, then my angel started drooping. When she led me up the stairs, I suspected we were headed for the Pearly Gates.

She opened the door.

46

I flicked on the lights. It was a little boy's room, with Lego monsters and kid-sized sports equipment and a Nerf basketball hoop.

Bethany turned the lights off. She sat on the bed. I sat next to her.

"So," I said.

She leaned against me with a sigh. "Yeah."

People downstairs broke into a round of applause.

She rubbed her hand up and down my arm. "I'm glad you came."

"You are?"

"Yep. Chip's not glad." She turned and looked at me, her eyes dark and serious in the glow of the Harry Potter alarm clock. "He thinks you're a loser."

"I get that a lot," I said.

This was so funny it sent her to the floor in giggles. When I helped her up, she somehow landed half on the bed, half in my lap.

Take me now, God, take me while it's perfect.

"Did you know that you used to sound like a chipmunk?"

Hold on, God.

"I did?"

"Oh, yeah. Remember? Earth science? Ninth grade. We used to laugh about it all the time."

"You mean you used to laugh at me."

"Well, yeah. But that was back when you were a dork." She ran her finger along my jaw. "You changed."

I took her hand in mine, turned it over, and kissed the palm. I was breathing hard and hoping she didn't notice. "I didn't change," I said. "Did I?"

She snorted. "Oh my God – you? You were, like, the quietest guy in our class, and *boom!* You surprised everyone."

"Getting arrested? That surprised me, too."

She snuggled (*yes! snuggled!*) against my shoulder for five full seconds. "When I saw you at my parents' party? Oh. My. God. Big difference. But you're still sweet, right?"

"That depends. Do you want me to be sweet?"

"Yes," she said with a grin. She reached up and brushed my hair out of my eyes. "Sweet and harmless and—" She pushed me down on the bed and pinned me in the hottest liplock of my life.

"Dangerous," she whispered.

My brain stopped functioning. My hormones kicked into overdrive and grabbed the steering wheel.

I was Wolfman, the Hulk, Casanova, the last man on earth with the last woman, ready and willing and very, very hot. Her lips were warm and sweet, and if her breath was a little nasty, well, that didn't bother my hard-on one bit. Her hand moved down my chest (*yes! yes!*) and she pressed herself against me and suddenly my arms were around her and the noise from the party was fading away and my hand traced the curve of her back and I realized that under her fairy leaf skirt she was wearing those tights and under those tights absolutely nothing and then, and then. . .

And then, because I suck, my brain came back to life.

And started wrestling with my hormones.

Brain: *You don't want this.*

Hormones: *Dude, this is EXACTLY what I want.*

B: *No, not like this—she's wasted.*

H: *What's your point?*

B: *She won't remember this, and if she does, she'll be angry.*

H: *Do you see where her hand is? God, that feels good. Can't you feel that?*

B: *She's drunk. You can't do this. It's wrong.*

H: *I want to do this.*

B: *Really? You want to go to school and say you scored with Bethany Milbury when she was so drunk she barely knew her name?*

H:

H:

H: *You're an asshole. I hate you.*

B: *She needs to eat something and drink some water. Don't let her drink any more beer.*

H:

H: *Yeah, I know.*

B: *She'll love you for taking care of her. She'll love that you respected her.*

H: *Five more minutes? Just five?*

B: *Now.*

H: *I can't believe you're making me do this.*

Yeah. I did it.

I rolled away from her. I counted to twenty. Then I counted to fifty. I sat up, carefully, and rebuckled my belt.

"Wha's wrong?" Bethany – sweet, wasted Bethany – muttered into the pillow.

"I want to see if they have any nachos. I love nachos, don't you?"

(H: *I cannot believe you just said that.*)

(B: *Shut the hell up.*)

"Don't you like me?"

I turned on the overhead light. "You know I do. I just . . . come on, let's go."

She squinted and held up her hand to shield her eyes from the light. "You're walking out on me?"

"No, it's not like that at all. It's just – look, Bethany, you're totalled. Shit-faced, no offence. You know I really like you and I want to be with you, but (*someone please shoot me now*) not like this."

She blinked and shook her head a little as the words sunk in. "You're blowing me off." She tried to stand up, lost her balance, and flopped on the bed. "I can't believe you're blowing me off."

When I reached out to help her she pulled away and

pouted. "What are you, too good for me? Gay? You don't like sex?"

"It's not that," I sighed. "Not at all. You don't get it."

"Oh, no, I totally get it." She stood up again, slower this time, and lurched towards the door. "You're weird, you know it, Tyler? I kinda liked you, because you're different, but you're not different, you're just weird." She steadied herself on the door frame. "Stupid freak."

47.

I followed her down the stairs. I was worried about her tripping, but it wouldn't have mattered because she would have fallen on piles of bodies. A couple hundred people had crammed inside. The party had turned into a tsunami of teenagers floating on noise, smoke, and beer.

I lost her in the crowd.

I could have stayed right behind her, I guess, but my stomach felt like she had just stomped on it with combat boots, and my hormones were ready to rip my brain out of its skull. I should have followed her because she wasn't thinking straight, and she looked innocent and vulnerable and she didn't know what she was saying or doing. But I didn't.

Yoda saw me wandering and had me follow him to the room where a bunch of guys were playing video games. I kept my eyes on the screen, but I wasn't really watching. He asked me what was wrong. I told him, for a change.

"Wow," he said.

"Exactly," I said.

"Do you want to get drunk?" he asked.

"Wouldn't help."

We turned to the game. Half an hour later, some girl I didn't know asked me if I had seen Bethany and I told her no. A few minutes after that, Hannah turned up.

"You need to talk to Bethany," she said.

"No way."

"She said you guys had a fight. She's upset."

"Good."

"What are you talking about?"

"Never mind. I'm not talking to her. You shouldn't, either. Let her solve her own problems."

The sound of breaking glass came from the living room, followed by angry voices.

Two bodies, fists flying, fell against the archway, bounced, then hit the floor. The crowd surged behind them, hollering and snapping photos.

Yoda and I hustled Hannah out the side door.

"We should go home," Yoda said.

Hannah frowned. "It's just getting good."

"It's only going to get worse," I said.

She looked back through the window, wincing as one of

the guys landed a punch on a fragile nose. "All right," she sighed. "Are you coming with us?"

I looked inside. No Bethany in sight. I had no obligations. She invited me, yeah, but then she blew me off. She could go home with her girlfriends or her brother. It was none of my business. She was none of my business.

"I'm going to stick around for a while," I said.

"Are you sure?"

"Yeah. We're not telling Mom about any of this, right?"

"Duh." Hannah gave me a quick peck on the cheek. "Love you, Ty. Stay out of trouble."

The power went out an hour later.

Some guy started screaming like a madman, running through the house telling everyone to get out. It was Josh Rawson. Yes, the party was at his house and, yes, his parents were in Jamaica, but Josh had been at a family dinner at his girlfriend's. That was him throwing the circuit breaker to cut off the electricity; that was him hollering and punching his buddies in the head.

When the lights were turned back on, I searched all over until I found Bethany curled up on the floor of the rec room. I shook her awake and told her we had to leave. She looked at me with confused, sleepy eyes. My stomped-on stomach fluttered.

"We have to go," I said gently. "They're kicking everybody out."

"Don' wanna," she pouted. She was beyond wasted – she was headed for incoherent.

"We don't have a choice."

I helped Bethany to her feet. She mumbled something about her shoes, but I had a bad feeling about where the night was headed, so I basically dragged her out to the curb.

Now what?

"Where's Stacey?" I asked. "Bethany, open your eyes. Where is Stacey? The girl you rode with?"

Her eyelids fluttered. "Left early. SAT prep."

"Great."

We were eight miles away from home, she was barefoot, and even with my jacket on over her sweatshirt, she was shivering. I could carry her, but eventually I'd collapse from exhaustion. She might be able to get enough warmth from my dying corpse until some early-morning commuter saw her and called an ambulance. She'd cry at my funeral and keep a bunch of silk flowers and a cross at the spot where I laid down my life for her.

That would work.

"No, wait." She started towards the road. "There's my brother. Chip! Chip!"

Chip was driving his Jeep along the white line on the side of the road at three miles an hour. He coasted to a stop on the shoulder, and Bethany opened the door.

I looked inside.

Crapcrapcrapcrap.

Chip smiled at me and passed out cold, his head on the steering wheel. Bethany didn't notice. She was already crawling into the backseat, where Parker Zithead was sitting, eyes unfocused.

It wasn't a hard decision.

I dragged Chip out, marched him around the car, and poured him into the passenger seat. I took the driver's seat. I buckled the seat belt and turned the key. So the night hadn't turned out the way I'd planned. It had turned out better, because I was a stand-up guy, righteous. When she sobered up, Bethany would realize that. Even Chip would have to back off, because I pulled his nuts out of the fire by getting him and his Jeep home in one piece.

The first mile went well. Then Chip began moaning – those deep, low, guy moans that meant he was in serious pain and about to—

—yep, puke his guts out in the foot well.

I rolled my window down and tried breathing through my mouth. Chip moaned again, leaned forward, and passed out with his head against the dashboard.

I glanced in the rearview mirror to see if the Zithead was going to blow, too.

I hit the brakes.

Bethany had crawled into Parker's lap. They were playing tonsil hockey, with her hands in his hair and his hands where I couldn't see them.

"Hey!" I screamed. "Leave her alone." I yanked the car to

the side of the road and threw it into park. I spun around in my seat and tried to peel Parker's arms off the body of my angel. "Get your goddamn hands off her, you pig!"

They separated with a loud smack of their lips.

"Wha'?" Bethany slurred.

"Don't do this, OK?" I asked. "Just – let me get you home."

She gave me the finger, turned, and attacked Parker's face again. Parker chuckled.

I pulled in the Milburys' driveway at 3:47 in the morning. I shut off the engine, got out, and threw the keys on the roof of the house. Chip was snoring, his chin against his chest. His shirt was disgusting.

Bethany and Parker were still at it. The back window was completely fogged up. They hadn't noticed that the car had stopped.

I thought about getting back in the car and driving it into a concrete pillar at ninety miles an hour.

But I had thrown away the keys.

48.

I existed on cruise control all weekend – home, bed, sleep, shower, looked at food, threw food out, bed again, stared at ceiling.

Nothing worked. The short independent film *Bethany Milbury Hates Tyler Miller* was playing on a constant loop in my head. I tried everything to drive it out: watched MTV, did a thousand jumping jacks and five hundred sit-ups, listened to music as loud as the volume dial would let me. I even tried beating my head against the wall. It left a dent, but it didn't stop her voice mocking me, her fingers in his hair.

I didn't bother with a jacket. If I was lucky, I'd catch pneumonia and die before dinner. As I walked through the gates of the Eternal Rest Cemetery, a flock of crows exploded out of a tree. It was just a matter of time before one of them dropped a depth charge on my head. I did not pull up the hood of my sweatshirt.

The crows followed me up the hill.

Grandpa Miller had been a travelling salesman, selling seeds and equipment to farmers. He got screwed out of a John Deere franchise back in 1965 and never got over it.

He picked out the plot himself, at the top of the hill. Grandma was not next to him. Forty years of marriage was bad enough, she said. She'd rather spend eternity alone.

The crows called back and forth. The trees shivered. The wind was blowing a cold front across the graves, preparing us for winter. When the nursing home called to tell Dad that Grandpa had finally died a couple years ago, he hung up the phone and said, "Thank God."

I sat on the damp ground next to his grave. His stone was white as bone and as hard as he was. It was so freaking pathetic that this was the only place I could think of to visit.

*

I cried like maybe it might help something.

It didn't.

49

By Monday morning I had almost convinced myself that a) it hadn't happened, or b) if it had happened, everyone concerned was so drunk they wouldn't remember, or c) if they remembered, they'd be too embarrassed to talk about it.

It's going to be great; everything is fine. I'll say something clever and witty to show that she hadn't hurt me at all – no, that's not my heart's blood dripping on the floor. Bethany who? Yeah, she was hot for me, but I had to let her down gently. You know. She's not really my type.

I cut homeroom.

A hall monitor caught me hiding in the men's room and wrote me up.

In calc we had a pop quiz, which we then got to trade with our "neighbour" for an instant jolt of public shame. I got a 37.

I kicked a soccer ball a little too hard in gym. It nailed some guy in the stomach and he had to go to the nurse. I didn't do it on purpose, but the teacher still yelled at me.

Viral rumors about the party were incubating in the halls. They said a gang fight broke out. They said the house almost burned down. They said Bethany Milbury blew me off in a major way. They said I was one of the kids who went to the hospital with alcohol poisoning. They said Josh's parents were sending him to military school.

They said there was another party, a bigger one, this coming Saturday.

My head hurt so much by the time English started, I had to keep it on my desk. Mr Salvatore was not sympathetic. He was all fired up about a few papers that turned out to be word-for-word identical. I tried to listen but all I heard was "plagiarism," "academic integrity," and "cheating" fifty million times.

Nobody looked him in the eye.

When he had worked himself up to the point where it looked like he might punch the whiteboard, he handed back our papers, announcing who had earned zeroes because they cheated. I hadn't copied my essay, honest. It compared the themes of *Paradise Lost* to *Crime and Punishment* and came in at exactly five hundred words.

He stood over me, essay in hand. I had a zero, too. "Time to start playing by college rules, Mr Miller. You need to actually read the book before you pretend you know what it's about."

My mouth opened up before my brain kicked into gear. "In college the teachers don't care if you show up to class as long as you pass the final. Do we get to play by that rule, too?"

The class went quiet.

Mr Salvatore licked his lips. "Are you asking for detention, Mr Miller?"

Choice: say "yes" and pay for it, or say "no" and look like a weenie.

"No."

"Have your parents sign your paper. And don't forge their signatures, OK? Be a man."

I waited until he launched into a discussion about the layers of meaning in *Punishment*, then I raised my hand and said I felt sick. When I walked in the nurse's office, the kid I hurt with the soccer ball (by accident, I swear, I swear) freaked out. The nurse gave me two Tums and a hall pass and made me leave.

The bell rang. Eleven o'clock and I'd already gone three rounds with a heavyweight without headgear. I cut lunch. I cut French, too.

Didn't cut study hall. Not much point in that. I sat next to the window and watched the wind stripping leaves off the trees.

The attendance office called me down at the end of the period. I was hoping that they'd punish me by chopping off my head in the courtyard, but no. I was instructed to serve detention for cutting my morning classes.

I ran into Bethany as I came out of the office. Literally. The bell had rung, the halls were packed, and I misjudged my entry into the traffic flow. We smacked into each other right in front of the glass walls. She dropped her books, and I bent down to pick them up before it registered what I was doing.

"Oh," she said.

"Yeah." I handed the books to her.

She turned her head away. "Thanks. See ya."

They were watching, the kids who fed the rumour mill. I should have walked away right then, right there. If we had been alone, maybe I would have. But they were watching.

"See ya."

I was a train wreck with a runaway mouth.

"Did you have a good time at the party?" I called.

She clutched her books tightly and walked down the hall.

I followed. "I mean, what was it you loved the most? Was it drinking yourself blind or throwing yourself on every guy there?"

She sped up, bumping into people at their lockers.

"How many guys did you drag upstairs, huh?" My voice cracked.

Bethany did a one-eighty in the middle of the hall and headed back the direction we came from. "Leave me alone," she said loudly.

"That's not what you said Friday night!"

"Leave me alone!"

People were openly staring, circling, taking bets.

Chip Milbury peeled off a group of guys coming out of the stairwell by the office. He looked at me, at his sister, then back at me again. "What's going on?"

Bethany ran over to him and said something under her breath. Chip glared at me. "Where do you get off talking to my sister like that?"

Mr Hughes stepped out of the office. The voices in the hall died down. "Is there a problem here?"

"This guy is harassing Bethany," Chip said.

Mr Hughes motioned to the crowd. "Go on, everyone, that was the bell. Nothing is happening here. Move along. You three, get to class. We'll sort this out later."

I caught a glimpse of Bethany's face just then. There were tears in her eyes, real tears, because I had hurt her, I had been a jerk, I was scum. She wiped the tears away with the palm of her hand and disappeared down the hall.

50.

I went to Hell right after dinner.

Level Twenty-Nine and rapidly descending. Like most games, Tophet was a test. You had to suffer through weeks of mind-numbing boredom on the early levels to get to the real deal. I was ready.

Gormley had finally stolen enough of Mammon's fortune that he could buy the protection he needed to blast through the Shields of Moloch. If this kept up, I'd be battling the Lord of Darkness within days.

Hannah burst into my room, shoved me off my keyboard, and opened a browser window.

"Hey!" I said. "I'm about to napalm a horde of succubus."

She concentrated on typing. "Shut up and watch." She hit the ENTER key and stood back.

The browser screen went black for a second, then three small photos popped up, and above them, the word SLUT.

"What's that?" I asked.

"Take a deep breath, Tyler." She clicked on the first photo and it enlarged.

Bethany. My Bethany. The quality of the picture was poor, but that was definitely her face. It was Bethany on a bed, wearing that little leaf skirt from her Halloween costume and a bra. That was all she was wearing. No tights, no sweatshirt. No wings. She was curled up in a ball, her hair spread out on the pillow, her eyes closed.

Hannah clicked on the next photo.

Almost the same pose, except the bra was missing.

"Oh, God," I muttered.

"Yeah," she said grimly. She clicked.

I only looked for a second, but I'd never forget. It was her and she was naked, turned on her side so that some things were covered by shadows. Her eyes were closed. A guy's hand was at the side of the shot, reaching for her butt.

"Who did this?" I asked.

"I don't know," she said.

"Call Yoda. He'll figure it out."

"Why do you care?" she asked. "I thought she blew you off."

"How do you know that?"

"Dude, she told the whole world."

I clicked on the browser window to close it. "How'd you find this?"

"Somebody IMed me the link." Hannah stood up. "Sucks to be her."

51.

Bethany did not go to school on Tuesday.

They said she did the whole team. It didn't matter the sport. The whole team.

They said she posed.

They said there was a secret website that showed every girl at the party on that bed.

They said it was a hoax.

They said the FBI was investigating.

They said she was dead.

They said she engineered the whole thing herself to get into *Playboy*.

Or to get out of midterms.

They said she drank so much that she fried her brain and was on life support.

They said she left the party in an ambulance.

They said she had it coming.

They said her brother was going to kill whoever took the pictures. He wasn't in school on Tuesday, either.

I tried. I butted my way into conversations all day long, in the halls, lunch line, at the urinals. I wrote notes. I whispered during the alienation lecture in English. I was yelled at in French, in French. I told everyone that I drove Bethany home. I said she was with me all night long. I said the whole thing had to be fake.

By the end of the day, they were saying that I did it.

52.

They called me down first period on Wednesday.

I didn't do it. I couldn't have. Wouldn't have. No way. No how.

I kept telling myself that over and over as I walked to my doom, to Mr Hughes's office. Every door I passed was open. Thousands of eyes watched me.

I did it, they said. I couldn't have done it. I wouldn't have. But I was the one who destroyed the school. No. No, I didn't.

It was just some spray paint. And I did not take her picture. God, if I had I wouldn't have shown it to anyone. I'd never put it on the Net. I mean, I'd thought about her looking like that, lying like that. But no. I did not take a picture. And I didn't destroy the school, either. It was just spray paint.

Mr Hughes's mouth moved, chewing through the air and the seriousness of the situation. I nodded when I was supposed to nod and shook my head when that seemed like the right thing to do. No, I didn't know anything about this, no sir, not a thing. I couldn't have done it, sir.

I did not hurt Bethany. I knew that.

But nobody else did.

53.

They said I was taken out of school in handcuffs again, but that should show you they didn't know squat. I went home, normal time, in Yoda's car. Yoda spent the whole ride home BSing me with one hundred reasons why nobody thought I pornogrified the girl of my dreams.

The cops showed up at eight thirty that night, just as Dad was about to eat the reheated leftover take-out enchiladas. I was watching television with Mom. Hannah was the one who sprinted to the answer the doorbell.

"The police are here," she said.

"What?" Mom asked.

I looked in the kitchen. Dad was at the table, his briefcase open on the chair next to him. He had some papers in one hand and a forkful of enchilada in the other.

He dropped the fork. "Don't let them in!" he said.

"What's going on?" Mom asked.

Dad pushed away from the table and went to the door. "Everybody stay there."

Hannah sat down on the couch without looking at me. I studied the rug. If I could tear through it with my bare hands, then rip through the wood underneath, I could squeeze through the hole in the floor, drop down to the basement, wiggle out one of the tiny basement windows (maybe), and take off before the cops even got inside.

Dad walked back in. "Hannah, go upstairs. Linda, Tyler, come with me."

We sat in the living room, the room in which no living was ever done except for dusting the piano, vacuuming the lemon-coloured carpet, and entertaining people we didn't like. Police officers, for example.

Officer Adams walked like his feet hurt. He was Dad's age, but he still had his hair. He was taller than Dad but looked underfed and tired. Mr Benson, my probation officer, was with him. The look he gave me when he walked in the door made me want to dig a hole through the floor again.

Mom's smile looked like the kind you see on a mummy, when the skin has shrunk so far you can see the teeth and gums. She was having a hard time speaking.

"Have a seat, gentlemen," Dad said.

Adams and Benson sat in the white, stuffed chairs. Mom and Dad sat on the couch under the framed print of *The Starry Night*. I sat on the piano bench. Hannah was sitting on the stairs, just high enough that Mom and Dad couldn't see her.

Dad opened his mouth, but Officer Adams jumped in first. "I know you folks must be nervous."

Mom squeaked. Dad put his hand on top of hers and patted it.

"But," Adams continued, "we're just looking for information."

That was cop-speak for "we have all of the information we need to send your son away to federal penitentiary for twenty years, but we'll save the taxpayers a lot of money if we can squeeze a confession out of him right here."

"Of course," Dad said.

"We're investigating an incident that took place at a party Friday night. A young woman, apparently under the influence of alcohol and or drugs, was stripped naked and photographed. Those pictures were then posted to the Internet."

Mom tried to squeak again, but no sound came out.

"That's a terrible thing," Dad said. "But I fail to see any connection to our family. Tyler wasn't at any party. He's still under the curfew imposed by the judge in May."

Mr Benson's eyes darted to me. I wondered if it would be possible to crawl into the piano and close the lid. Maybe the wires would cut me into hundreds of pieces and I would bleed out before anyone noticed.

Adams nodded. "Well, sir, we're at the beginning of this investigation, but it's clear that your son was indeed at the party, according to" – he paused to flip through the pages of his notebook – "according to seven witnesses. Your daughter, Hannah, was there, too."

There was the sound of clumping feet running up the stairs, down the hall, and then a door slamming.

"Ah," Dad said.

Adams turned to me. "You were at the party, right, Tyler?"

I nodded.

"And by that nod, you mean yes?"

"Yes, sir."

He asked a bunch of boring questions – how did I hear about the party (*everybody knew about it*), how much did I drink (*one sip doesn't count*), how much did I smoke (*nothing*), how many people were there (*lost count*), how did I get there (*walked*).

"You walked?" Benson interrupted.

"Yes, sir."

"We don't let him drive any more," Mom explained.

Adams cleared his throat and turned the page in his notebook. "In which room did you take the photographs?"

"I didn't take any pictures," I said.

"In which room did you have sex with Bethany Milbury?"

Crapcrapcrap.

"We didn't have sex."

"Bethany Milbury!" Dad roared. "Is that who we're talking about? Christ Almighty, Tyler, what were you thinking?"

"Please, Mr Miller," Benson said. "Sit down."

"Would you like a minute to compose yourself?" Adams asked.

"No," barked Dad. Wisps of smoke trailed out of his nose and mouth as he sat. "Go on."

"Did you go into a bedroom with Bethany?"

The sound of metal doors locking. "Yes."

"Were you alone in the room with her?"

Older inmates. Big, older inmates. With gang tattoos. "Yes."

"Was she drunk?"

"She had a beer in her hand. I got there late. I don't know how much she had to drink."

"What happened when the two of you were alone in the bedroom?"

I looked down. The laces of my sneakers were frayed. "We talked, mostly. I was at the party because she invited me. I thought . . . I thought she liked me. So we talked."

Adams was staring at me. "What kind of physical contact did you have with her?"

My mother was sitting very still.

142

"Tyler?" Adams repeated.

"Not much." I cleared my throat. "She came on to me – we kissed. She wanted to do more, but I didn't. I mean, no, I did, but I didn't, not like that, not there, not when she was—"

"Drunk?" Adams asked.

"Yeah. Drunk. So I blew her off and she got mad. She said some bitchy things and took off. I didn't see her until the party ended." I explained where I found her and how she was dressed. Mom stopped looking at me. Dad didn't.

Adams finished writing and spent a long minute reviewing his notes. "How long have you been stalking her?"

"What?" I looked up. "I haven't been stalking her. I was trying to protect her. The only reason I stayed was to keep an eye on her because everybody was so trashed."

"If you were keeping an eye on her," Benson interrupted, "then how did those pictures get taken?"

Adams waved him off. "Were you responsible for a serious accident on August the twenty-eighth, during which Bethany suffered severe lacerations on the bottom of her foot, which necessitated a trip to the hospital and multiple stitches?"

"It was an accident!" My voice was panicked. I had no control over it. "Chip shoved me. I couldn't help it."

"Did you verbally harass her in school on Monday afternoon?"

"Who told you that?"

"That's enough, Tyler," Dad said. "Settle down."

Benson closed his eyes and shook his head.

143

"Are you going to arrest my son?" Dad asked.

"Not tonight," Adams said. "But when we do, he's looking at felony charges that could include lewd behaviour, forcible touching, sexual harassment, sexual misconduct, all kinds of voyeurism counts, and possibly a kidnapping charge."

Kidnapping? I couldn't even get the word out.

"OK, good job," Dad said. "You've terrified him – congratulations. We both know you can lie about anything you want right now, so let's cut to it. What evidence do you have?"

"We've talked to a number of students—"

"*Ev-i-dence*," Dad said slowly. His yellow dragon eyes flashed at Adams. "Aside from rumours spread by drunken morons, what makes you believe my son did anything beside break curfew?"

"Did Bethany accuse Tyler?" Mom asked. "Was she—?"

Adams thought for a moment before he answered. "There is no medical evidence that she has ever had intercourse. And she claims her memory of the incident is spotty. We're starting with the photographs."

It hit me. "I don't have a camera," I said. "How could I take her picture without a camera?"

"We believe the photographs were taken with a camera phone," Adams said.

"Tyler doesn't have a phone," Mom said.

"He doesn't?" Adams asked.

"We took it away when the first thing happened," Mom explained.

"He could have used anyone's phone," Adams said. "We're investigating the possibility of co-conspirators."

Dad interrupted. "But the point is you have no evidence. I want to see this website."

"It's been taken down, Mr Miller. It was up for approximately four hours."

"So how do you know that a crime was even committed?"

"Numerous students printed the images."

Ouch.

"We'd like to borrow Tyler's computer," Adams said.

"Why?" I asked.

"Our experts will be able to tell if your computer was used to upload, store, or download the images."

"I didn't. I mean, Hannah showed me the site last night; you'll see that in the browser history. But I didn't do it. My computer will prove it, so yeah, take it."

"How do we know you won't set him up?" Dad asked. "What if you guys think he is the easiest kid to nail for this, and you'll doctor his computer to prove it?"

"I can come back with a warrant," Adams said.

This is not happening. My dad is not going toe-to-toe with a cop, defending me like he cares. I am not a suspect. Nobody did anything criminal to Bethany. In fact, the party never happened.

"I'll take you to his room," Dad said.

I stayed on the bench while Dad supervised the removal of my computer. Mr Benson carried it, component by component, to the squad car while Adams interviewed Hannah in her room, with Mom standing guard. Hannah was bawling. She always cried when she got caught.

As Adams and Benson pulled out of the driveway, Dad watched through the living-room curtains. I hadn't moved. Mom was still upstairs with Hannah, who had cranked it up to a full-blown wail.

I knew what was coming.

Dad snapped the curtains shut. He stood in the middle of the lemon-yellow carpet, opened his jaws, and sprayed fire everywhere. I was a loser, a liar, a jerk, an idiot, a disgrace, and an embarrassment. I had cost the family a fortune in lawyer's fees already. I had ruined the family's good name, my father could barely hold his head up at work, and now this—

Breathe. Breathe.

"—this is the last straw, Tyler. Brice Milbury will fire me and blacken my name. I've worked twenty-seven years to get where I am, and you just blew it all to hell, because you had a hard-on for some drunken little bitch."

"Don't call her that," I said.

"Look at me when I'm talking to you! I never thought I'd say this, but I wish you took drugs. If you were high, I could blame it on that. But no, you screw up just for the joy of it—"

I tuned out again. He kept at it for another hour or so,

flapping his wings and tearing at the sky with his talons. He was done with me. Done. If they arrested me, he'd kick me out of the house. He blamed me for Mom's migraines and his blood pressure. He blamed me for my bad grades, my bad attitude, and my bad haircut. I was also responsible for the price of gas, global warming, and the national debt.

My butt fell asleep. That piano bench was hard. No wonder Hannah and I quit lessons when we were little. As he paced back and forth, I studied the family Christmas photos behind him, and the spots where the wallpaper seams had separated.

The furnace kicked on, blowing that faint mouldy smell across the vacuum-cleaner lines at the edge of the lemon-yellow carpet, across the strings inside the piano, across the laces of my sneakers.

Dad's nose twitched. He stuttered once, then shouted, "Go to your room!"

I stopped in the upstairs bathroom, popped four ibuprofen, and chugged half a bottle of NyQuil. Then I went to bed like the bad little boy I was.

54.

The sound of my parents yelling at each other woke me up at one thirty. It was an All-Star cage match: Out-of-Control Dadman versus the GinandTonica Momster.

Hannah slipped into my room. "I can't sleep."

"I wonder why," I said.

It had been a long time, but we both knew the routine. I pulled out the sleeping bag from the top shelf of my closet. Hannah crawled into my bed. She had her old Raggedy Ann with her. That's the kind of thing brothers don't tell about sisters. I tucked the covers under her chin.

"Thanks, Tyler," she said.

"Yeah." I unrolled the sleeping bag on the floor and got in. Mom and Dad were still at it downstairs. Their vocal cords were made of leather. After a while it faded back into a green NyQuil haze, thunder booming on the other side of a hill.

"Ty?"

"What?"

"This is going to get better, right?"

"Right," I lied.

"Ty?"

"I'm trying to go to sleep, Hannah."

"I know you didn't do it."

I rolled over. "Thanks."

55.

All the crap I had endured up until then – the face flushes in middle school, the wedgies, the names, being ignored, mocked, teased, spit on, even being hurt by Bethany – that stuff was all kindergarten. This was big league.

Every step in a crowded hall came with a shove, a trip, a couple of quick shots to the kidneys. By lunchtime my notebooks were in shreds, my wallet had been stolen, and my watch was in a million pieces in the math wing. A couple of teachers saw it. They saw it and they saw nothing.

I thought about walking out the front door, just walking, but that would have been a giant admission of guilt, and I was still stupid enough to think it mattered.

Hannah looked me over as I sat down in the cafeteria. "That bad, huh?"

"Worse. You?"

"I'm OK." Her eyes were still swollen from crying and arguing with Mom the night before.

"Don't worry," Yoda said. "They'll figure out who did it, and everybody will chill."

"Thank you for lying," I said. "I feel better now."

"And Bethany will find out that you are not an evil, perverted stalker, and you guys can hook up again."

"Are you high?" I asked him. "I'm toast. Done. *Fini.*"

Hannah dipped a carrot stick in a cup of ranch dressing. "Leave Calvin alone. He's in shock. He can't believe that Mom grounded me until graduation."

"I'm not even allowed to call her," Yoda said.

Hannah laid her head on his shoulder. "We'll figure something out."

149

"Don't worry," I said. "Sneaking out to a party is nothing like committing a dozen felonies on the boss's daughter. If I get arrested, they'll forget all about grounding you."

"The police won't arrest you, because you didn't do it." She bit the carrot. "Stop being so negative."

"I'm going to be arrested, tried, convicted – for something I didn't do – sent to jail where I will become the girlfriend of a large, scary man, and where I will also develop an addiction to . . . I don't know, sniffing bleach or something."

"Sniffing bleach will kill you," Yoda pointed out.

I picked up the fork from Hannah's tray. "Then sign me up. Bethany Milbury will never look at me again. In fact, she'll forget I ever existed."

Hannah let out a long and dramatic sigh. Yoda and I waited.

"OK," she started. "I hate to be the one to break this to you, but—"

"My life is over? I know that, thanks."

"No, listen. This Bethany thing? You never had a chance."

"What are you talking about? She likes me. Well, she *liked* me. Past tense."

"It wouldn't have worked," Hannah explained.

I tried to stab the fork into the table. "What's that supposed to mean?"

Yoda shook his head a little, trying to get her to back down. She ignored him.

"Bethany is popular, Ty." She said it carefully, as if I had never heard of the concept.

"What's your point?"

"You aren't."

Yoda tried a diversion. "I've never understood what makes the popular kids popular. It must be a hive activity, a neurochemical message that all hive members receive, but no one understands."

"We're not bees," I pointed out.

"It's not that complicated," Hannah said. "The popular kids aren't really popular. They're obnoxiously loud, good-looking, and rich. Nobody likes them, but they rule the place."

"And everybody wants to be them," Yoda pointed out.

"Well, duh. When a non-popular kid tries to cross the line, like Ty, bad things happen. You can't mate a dog with a racehorse. Give me that fork before you hurt yourself."

They talked about nothing and cuddled for the rest of the period. I drew small blue demons on my hand with a pen.

Somebody poured milk down my back when we were leaving.

56.

Bethany turned up in school for the first time on Friday. She was wearing her black turtleneck, tight black jeans, and new sneakers. She looked like she hadn't eaten in a month, and her eyes were swollen under the make-up.

They said that her parents were forcing her to go to school as punishment for going to the Rawson party.

Mr Hughes met me at the front door and informed me that "until the matter was resolved," I'd be spending homeroom in the main office.

"It would be best for everyone," he said. "I'm sure you understand."

Chip Milbury passed me in the hall on the way to first period. He pointed to his eyes, then at me.

Great. Chip was watching. Now my life was complete.

Mr Salvatore attacked me in English class. "What was Doctor Faustus tempted with, Tyler?" he asked. He was perched on a corner of his desk, smiling like he gave a damn.

"I don't know."

"What was the author, Marlowe, trying to tell us?"

"To pay attention in English class?"

A few people giggled. Salvatore stood up. "Did you read last night's assignment?"

Why was he always doing that? Say "yes," and I'd be hammered again. Say "no," and the same thing would happen.

I shrugged.

"Did anyone read last night's assignment?"

Everyone who was not me raised their hands.

"Someone please summarize *Doctor Faustus* for us," he said. As a girl sitting by the window explained, Mr Salvatore took a book from his desk, opened it, and set it on my desk. He patted me on the shoulder, twice, and went to the board, where he started scribbling.

I tried to read, but the letters kept moving around.

I stopped at my locker after English. Mistake. Something accidentally hit me on the right side of the head. It felt like the bumper of a pick-up truck.

Nobody saw anything.

The nurse gave me ice and called Mr Hughes. An hour later he joined me in the nurse's office and told me that I would be spending the rest of the day in study hall. He had already talked to my parents. They would be coming to school for a meeting on Monday.

If I hadn't been so tired, I might have said something.

I went to the study hall room and laid my head down on my books. A trickle of water leaked from the ice bag and escaped down the back of my neck.

As the day wore on, the room filled with bees and emptied, first buzzing, then silence, buzzing, silence, as the members of the hive flew through their rigid, patterned dances. The sound of their beating wings filled my mind and smothered it.

*

When I finally woke up, the room was empty except for Joe the janitor leaning against a mop and giving me the evil eye.

"Hey," I said. "Did I miss the bell?"

"Did you do what they say you did?" he asked.

"No."

He examined the end of the mop for splinters. "I didn't think so," he finally said. "Keep your chin up."

I laid my head back down until I heard him leave the room.

57.

After dinner that night we drove to the photography studio for our annual Christmas photo. We did not talk in the car.

Mr Gunnarson had a giant mirror on one wall of his studio. Mom dug a brush out of her purse and handed it to me without a word. After I brushed my hair, she handed me my brown felt antlers. I put them on. Mom and Hannah wore antlers, too, along with the stoned reindeer sweatshirts. I wore a red sweater.

Dad was in his suit. He refused to wear antlers, or even a Santa hat. He held the prop, an empty box covered with red-and-green wrapping paper, while sitting in the leather armchair in front of the fake fireplace. A plastic tree poked up at the back of the shot. We all gathered around Dad: Mom to his right, Hannah to the left, me behind the chair.

"No, no, no," Gunnarson scolded me. "Your head is too far off the ground. I can't get it in the frame. Let's try something else."

Four "something else"s later, we found the right combination: Mom perched lightly on the arm of the chair, Hannah hanging over the back, and me down on one knee to the left, like someone had just been injured on a soccer field. Dad held the empty present in his lap.

"Very festive," Gunnarson said, clicking away. "Say 'Peace.' That's it, big smiles. Peeeeeeace."

58.

Dad woke me up at seven o'clock Saturday morning.

"No sleeping in," he said. "I have chores for you."

It didn't take too long to climb the ladder and step onto the roof. I planted my butt on the shingles and inched my way up to the peak. An ugly-looking cloud bank was building in the west. The air smelled like winter.

The mail truck was coming down the street, dodging potholes. Our neighbours on either side – we never talked to them – had above-ground pools half-filled with stagnant water. The sidewalk in front of our house was more cracked than I remembered. I shuffled my boots back and forth on a loose shingle.

I studied the Christmas lights that I was supposed to replace. Mom had tried to yank them down, but they wouldn't budge. From up here, the problem was obvious. After Dad looped the wires over nails he had driven into the roof, he had bent the nails over, so that the lights wouldn't blow down in a strong wind. Which is why he hadn't taken them down himself: good idea, bad execution, difficult clean-up job. Story of his life.

And I had forgotten to bring up a pair of pliers or a claw hammer. Bad idea, no preparation, giant mess. Story of my life.

Dad came out of the house, shielded his eyes from the sun, and looked up at me. "How long will it take? I need you to help me down here."

"I need a pair of pliers."

"You didn't bring them up with you? Hold on."

It only took him a second to find them, and he was back out of the garage. He stood below me. "Catch."

"No. Wait!"

The pliers bounced off the roof, hit the gutter, and dropped back to the ground.

"I'll come down," I said. "I have to go to the bathroom anyway."

"No, no. You stay put. I'll bring them up." Dad stuck the pliers in his back pocket, pushed up his sleeves, and blew out a sharp blast of air as he put his hand on a rung above his head.

"Want me to hold it?" I asked.

"I'm fine." He climbed five feet off the ground, pulled out the pliers, and held them up. "If you lean down, you should be able to reach them."

I stretched on my stomach, toes dug in for grip, but he was too far away. "You have to come up a couple more rungs at least, Dad. Or I can come down the ladder."

He frowned, but he put the pliers back in his pocket and climbed, one shaky step after the next.

"Lean your weight towards the house," I suggested.

He didn't say anything, but he leaned and climbed three more rungs, until his head popped over the edge of the roof. There was sweat coating his upper lip, and he was breathing like he just ran the 400.

"Didn't think I could do it, did you?" He held on to the ladder with a death grip, reached into his pocket in slow motion, then handed the pliers to me.

"Thanks," I said.

"Don't mention it." He glanced around. "I forgot how nice the view is from up here. A man should climb on his roof more often."

"Yeah."

"Indeed." He nodded like we were having an everyday conversation, just two regular guys twenty feet in the air. "It is a nice view."

He glanced down, then leaned closer to the ladder.

"Do you need something else?" I asked.

He cleared his throat. "Your mother . . . I'm supposed to

talk to you. She thinks I was too hard on you the other night. After the police left."

I scratched at a spot of rust on the pliers.

"I was upset," he said. "We were all upset."

"That's putting it mildly."

"About Bethany," he started. "You could have taken advantage of that situation."

"Totally."

"Why didn't you?"

I grabbed a nail with the pliers and twisted it, freeing the strand of Christmas lights. "It would have been wrong."

The wind blew through the naked branches of the maple trees, tangled in the strands of Dad's comb-over, and teased them up straight. He smelled a little, the old-guy smell of dirty socks and underwear sweat. There were black smudges under his eyes.

"I'm proud of you for that, Tyler," he said. "I just wish you could have applied that thinking to the entire incident."

I resisted the temptation to shove the ladder away from the house and send him plunging to the ground.

He eyed the Christmas lights. "How long will this take?"

"Twenty minutes, tops, but I need a pit stop first. I drank a lot of juice at breakfast."

He didn't move.

"Uh, Dad? You have to go down first," I said, "because you're on the ladder."

"Right."

I waited. "Is something wrong?" I asked.

He peered up at me, then at the ground again, and then at his hands, which were gripping the ladder so tightly, the tendons and veins looked like they had been carved out of a block of granite.

"I am experiencing vertigo."

"What does that mean?"

"I'm dizzy."

"Oh, man. OK. Well, I'll yell for Mom. She can hold the bottom of the ladder for you."

His eyes widened. "Don't you dare. I'll be fine."

It took me fifteen minutes to coax him down the ladder, one rung at a time: ". . .move your foot, Dad – no, a little to the left, feel it? Right there. Now move your hand. You have to let go of the ladder first. Right, that's good. No, don't look down. The ground is still there. Okay, next step. . ."

Once down, he stood on the lawn and watched me descend. Sweat trickled off his scalp. When I was on the ground, he said, "Thank you, son."

Officer Adams interviewed me the second time on Sunday. The interview was only "informational," he said. "A friendly discussion." We sat in our living room with my parents on the couch looking like they had forgotten their lines.

He asked the same questions.

I gave him the same answers.

I was beginning to think I needed a lawyer, but Dad said no, it would be an admission of guilt. He would handle it.

Mom gave Dad a look like she was ready to rip out his throat with her teeth.

59.

I stayed in Yoda's car during homeroom on Monday and signed in ten minutes after calc began. The call for me to go to Mr Hughes's office came half an hour into gym class, second period. Pissed me off. We were doing a personal-fitness unit. Most of the girls were yoga-ing and gossiping. Some guys were jogging laps. I had a corner all to myself where I alternated between sets of push-ups, sit-ups, and squats. The back of my shirt was dark with sweat, and the spot on my abs was growing.

I asked if I had time to change my clothes. The teacher said no.

The secretary waved me in with a nod of her head. She and I were going to be on a first-name basis soon.

I opened the door. Hughes looked up from his desk without smiling. So did my parents, sitting directly across from him in the nice chairs.

"Hi," I said.

"Have a seat," Mr Hughes said. "I was just telling your

parents how grateful I am that they took the time to come here personally and discuss the situation."

"Of course," Dad said.

Mom had a yellow pad on her lap and a pen in her right hand. I sat on the hard plastic chair under the clock.

Hughes started talking and blew a lot of smoke out of his butt, but what it boiled down to was this: he didn't know what to do with me.

"But he's not suspended," Dad pointed out.

"No," Hughes admitted.

"And you let him go to class this morning," Mom said. "Obviously."

"That was something of an oversight," Hughes said. "Tyler was supposed to report to the office when he arrived."

"So I'm in trouble for going to class?" I asked.

Hughes straightened his blotter. "I didn't say that. This is an unusual circumstance – one that, frankly, our handbook doesn't cover."

Mom leaned forward. "I must admit, I'm a little confused."

Dad's eyes rolled up to heaven just a fraction.

"Has Tyler broken any rules this semester?" she continued.

"No," Hughes admitted.

"And Officer Adams has explained that he has not been arrested."

"But the police are talking to him," Hughes said.

"The police are talking to a lot of kids," Dad said. "Why is Tyler the only one being singled out?"

"Because Tyler is the one we're worried about. I'm told there were several incidents last week, not just what happened on Friday. We want to protect him from students who may not yet understand the concept of innocent until proven guilty."

Mom nodded. She was scribbling on the pad as fast as I had ever seen anyone write.

"How will he keep up with his classes if you stuff him in isolation?" Dad asked. "This semester is critical to his chances of getting into the right school."

"His teachers have agreed to tutor him in their free periods and provide him with class notes, whatever he needs. We don't anticipate this will go on too long. A few days, maybe a week."

Mom raised her hand a little. "And why is it he can't stay at home, exactly?"

Hughes relaxed, now that it was clear that my parents weren't going to attack him. "Keeping him at home would have to be considered a suspension. We don't have the grounds for that. This compromise will work best for everyone concerned."

Dad glanced at the clock. Mom finished writing the last words that Hughes said, then raised her finger, said, "Hold on a sec," and drew a business card out of her purse. She stood slightly and passed it across the desk to Hughes. He read it with a frown.

"That's the name of my lawyer," Mom explained.

"You called Pete Satterfield?" Dad asked. "I told you we could handle this."

Mom smiled. "I didn't call Pete. That's from Hewson, Heiligman, and Keehn. *My* lawyers."

"Since when do you have a lawyer?"

Mom ignored the question. "I spoke to Jill Hewson this morning. She said to tell you that if you isolate Tyler and single him out for doing absolutely nothing, then you should notify the school district's attorney that we'll be filing suit for unlawfully denying him his education."

Dad threw his hands in the air. "For Christ's sake, Linda, they're trying to help him. Do you want him beat up every day?"

"Do we want our kids in a school that would allow that to happen?" she responded. She pointed at Hughes. "If you do this, you're admitting that you don't have control over your own students. How is that going to look in the newspaper?"

"Now, wait just a minute—" Hughes's face was turning red.

"You're way off base," Dad said.

"Excuse me," I tried.

Mom wasn't smiling any more. "My son has done nothing wrong."

"Hello?" I demanded. "Do I get an opinion here?"

They all turned to me.

"Of course you do," Mom said. Mr Hughes nodded.

"I don't mind it," I said. "If they want to put me in a study hall, or just take me out of class until this all dies down, I'm cool with it."

"Are you sure?" Mom asked.

"Yeah."

"This wouldn't be an excuse for you to slack off," Dad warned.

"Oh, God," Mom sighed.

"No, it's OK. Mr. Hughes is right." (Yeah, I said that.) "It's not worth the aggravation. And this is hard enough on Bethany. Maybe it'll be easier on her if I'm not around."

Dad smiled slightly at Mom.

"I don't want to cause trouble," I finished.

"Well, then," Hughes said.

"Are you sure?" Mom repeated. "Are you one hundred percent sure this is what you want?"

I shifted in my chair, pulling my sweat-sticky legs off the plastic. Dad glanced at the clock again.

"Yeah," I said.

Mom and Dad left in separate cars. Hughes gave me time to change back into my clothes and get my stuff out of my locker.

My new room was just down the hall from the administration office. It had a table and three chairs, an empty bookshelf, a trash can, and a door with a window in it. They used it for tutoring or as a holding cell, depending on the situation.

I opened my English book to finish the *Faustus* play. It was written in 1588.

Not marching in the fields of Thrasymene,
Where Mars did mate the warlike Carthagens;
Nor sporting in the dalliance of love,
In courts of kings where state is overturn'd;

Oh, yeah, that made sense.

The bell rang and the halls filled, then emptied. A few curious faces stared in at me. I could hear the whispers through the walls. They were saying that I was part of a network of Internet perverts.

They were saying that I had a trench coat.

They were saying that I was heavily medicated.

They were saying that the cops were looking at a couple of other guys, too.

But they were still saying I was a piece of garbage.

60.

Tuesday I sat on my chair at my table in my cell. Day two of limbo. In school, but not in school. Suspended, but not really. Every time the bell rang, kids passing in the hall would slap and kick my door. Every time it happened, I jumped.

I had been here before, stuck in between worlds. Last

spring, I was stuck in court limbo while the judge and the D.A. and Hughes threw dice to decide my fate. I'd spent weeks in Bethany limbo, wondering if she liked me.

Come to think of it, all of high school had been limbo – middle school, too. As soon as my zits popped – *wham* – drop Tyler Miller in limbo. Change the rules daily so he never knows how to act or talk or dress. Nail him with the longest, slowest puberty mankind has ever known. Let's see how much damage one dumb jerk will put up with before he snaps. That sounds like a fun game, doesn't it?

I translated ten pages of *L'Étranger* for French. They were absurd. I read the Constitution, too. Tried to translate it into French. That was ridiculous.

Yoda didn't kick my door. He knocked politely after the last bell rang, then opened it and stuck his head in. "Want to go to the mall?"

"With you and Hannah? No, thanks."

"She has weightlifting."

"And so you want to go to the mall alone? You never go to the mall alone."

"That's why I'm asking you. Come on. I need the moral support. I have to get a job."

He needed a job because my sister was expensive. She was still grounded, so he couldn't take her any place. Instead, he bought her presents. Lots of presents. His bank account was almost tapped out.

Yoda drove. He never shut up, going on and on about the road trip he was going to take with his parents, looking at colleges.

The mall looked like one of my mother's Christmas fantasies on steroids. The constant carolling made a headache stab at my brain stem with a collection of stainless-steel kitchen knives, $49.95, on sale.

Yoda collected applications from two department stores, a shoe store, the bookstore, and the kiosk that sold sausage and orange cheese. I thought that the people who handed him the applications were totally blowing him off, but he didn't think so. He was the polite job candidate, with copies of his transcript, four statements from personal references, and two recommendations from teachers.

I paged through one of his packets as we walked away from the kiosk. "Why didn't you ask Mr Pirelli for a reference?"

"He hates me because of the equipment I broke."

"No, he doesn't." I flipped to page three as we stepped on the escalator. "Nobody cares that you were a freshman library aide."

"Yes, they do," he said. "It shows initiative. You should try it some time."

"What's that supposed to mean?"

"It means I'm hungry. Taco Bell or King Wok?"

*

He bought four burritos with the extra-hot sauce. I bought something that had cheese in it. No hot sauce. My stomach was already on fire. My headache hovered around a Terrorist Threat intensity.

"Can we go?" I asked after he finished the second burrito.

"I'm not done yet."

"You could eat it in the car."

"Or I could eat it here." He unwrapped another one. "What's wrong?"

"That is the funniest question you've ever asked me. 'What's wrong?' I'll have to remember that."

"You know what I mean. Things are crappy, yeah, but I was asking, is there anything crappier than the rest?"

His phone rang. It was Hannah, so I ceased to exist for him.

I poured all of the hot-sauce packets onto the tray and sprinkled pepper in it.

Yoda laughed into the phone.

I studied the beams that arched high over the food court. A lost balloon floated up and bounced between them. A kid wailed.

I could see myself hanging from a rope tied to the beams, tongue sticking out, legs dangling in the air. But it would be hard to get up there without anyone noticing.

"Hey!" Yoda waved his phone an inch from my nose. "Wake up. Want to talk to your sister?"

"No."

The kid pointing to his balloon stomped his feet and cried louder. He had a snotty nose and was stuffed into a winter jacket. His mother was focused on cramming as much pizza into her mouth as humanly possible. The red balloon bounced along the ceiling.

"Come o-o-o-on," Yoda whined. He shoved the phone in my face again. "Talk to her or she'll be mad at me."

I smacked the phone out of his hand. It hit the floor and skittered to the wall. The battery popped off.

Yoda didn't move. I stood up, walked over, picked up the two pieces, and brought them back to the table. I replaced the battery and turned the phone back on. I didn't look at him when I gave it back.

"Still works," I said. "Sorry."

He rubbed a scratch on the cover of the phone with his thumb. "Why did you do that?"

The kid alternated between wailing and sobbing.

"I don't know," I said.

"I'm just trying to help."

"Yeah, well, don't. It just makes it worse. Everyone acting like everything is normal, you laughing on the phone, handing out résumés."

"What do you want me to do?"

"Erase the last ten days of my life."

"Impossible, that is."

I stood up. The boy was punching his mother's leg and

screaming so loud I thought all of the glass in the mall would shatter.

"Can't you shut that kid up?" I hollered.

Everyone in the food court stopped talking and stared at me. A new song came on the loudspeaker, "Silent Night."

Yoda put his last burrito in the bag and picked up the tray.

"What are you doing?" I asked.

"We're going home."

"Make up your mind. You want to stay. You want to go. What's it going to be?"

He carried the tray to the trash can, pushed the papers in, wiped up the hot-sauce mess with a napkin, and put the tray on top. He walked back to my side of the table. People had stopped staring. Now they were whispering to each other.

"I'm trying to help you," Yoda said quietly.

"You're trying to stay on my good side so you can get into my sister's pants."

He took a deep breath. He flipped open his cell phone, brushed off some dust that wasn't there, then closed it and stuck it into his pocket.

"At some point, you're going to feel like a real asshole for saying that to me," he said. "When that happens, you give me a call."

As he disappeared down the escalator, that stupid kid finally stopped crying.

61

Yoda and his parents left for Kent State, Case Western, and OSU on Wednesday. Hannah and I rode the bus to school.

She did not sit with me.

I spent most of the day reading the entire US gov textbook. I highlighted it, too. What were they going to do? Suspend me? Arrest me?

Mr Salvatore dropped by during his lunch break and explained *Faustus*. I told him that Marlowe should have written it the way he explained it. Mr S. thought that was funny. He pointed to a line in the play, towards the end, when Dr Faustus is about to sign over his soul to the devil. "Do you know what means?"

"*Homo, fuge*? That he's gay?"

"Don't be an idiot. It's Latin. *Homo* means man, *fuge*, fly, so 'fly, oh man,' or 'fly away.' God is speaking to him, dropping a giant hint that he should take off, follow the light, if you will; do something positive instead of sealing the deal with the devil."

"So this is really important?"

"You could say that, yeah."

I made a quick note of the page number. "Why did the guy write it in Latin? He's making the most important stuff the hardest to understand."

"But you won't forget it, will you?"

"Huh?"

"Because it's in Latin, because it's different and hard, you'll remember it. A friend of mine in grad school had that tattooed on his arm. Kept him out of trouble, he said."

"No offence, but you had some weird friends."

"It was grad school, what can I say? See if you can write that essay now."

Somebody put a doughnut on my table when I was in the john taking a leak. It was a peanut-butter-and-jelly doughnut. It could have been either Joe or Toothless. Dopey didn't share.

I must have nodded off doing calculus, chair leaning against the wall, arms crossed over my chest, thin strand of drool on my chin. It was hot in there. No windows.

I woke up when I heard the door open, the slow *cli-click* of the handle turning, the latch releasing. I opened my eyes and wiped my chin.

I froze.

Bethany was standing just outside my door.

She was wearing a pair of faded jeans, a light-blue turtleneck, and a baggy gray Warriors hoodie. Her hair was in a braid down her back. Her left arm was curled around a stack of books. Her blue purse was over her right shoulder. She didn't have on any makeup or earrings. She looked like she was twelve.

Imagine you're sitting in your living room watching ESPN, and you look up and a deer has wandered in. She's shaking. Her legs are like twigs and her eyes so big you can see yourself in them. You're afraid that if you move, or say anything, she'll panic and run through the sliding-glass door, but if you don't move, or say anything, she'll walk away again.

"I'm sorry," she whispers.

I sit silent, a rock.

She sighs. "You're still mad at me. I don't blame you. I was a bitch." She wipes the tears off her face. "I hope someday you'll forgive me. . ."

I stand up, throw the chair aside. I walk towards her.

She didn't say a word. She didn't even come in, just stayed there in the hall with her hand on the doorknob.

I almost said something, but the bell rang.

Officer Adams showed up again at eight o'clock that night, and we all assumed our positions: cop in the chair, me on the bench, parents on the couch.

Dad was sitting square under the van Gogh print this time, directly across from me. He frowned. The creases in his forehead deepened into canyons.

Adams asked the same questions and I gave the same answers for ten minutes.

We were all confused when Mom left the room and came back holding her purse. That wasn't in the script. She whipped out another one of her lawyer's cards.

"The interview is over," she said. "Call this number if you have any other questions."

173

Adams took the card.

"Let me walk you to the door," Mom said.

After the cops left, Dad poured himself a scotch. He made a gin and tonic for Mom, who had curled up on the couch with the remote and a photo-supply cataloge.

"No, thanks," she said, turning a page.

"What?" Dad said.

"I don't want one."

"You don't want a drink?"

"Actually, I do." She stood up and tossed me the remote before she walked into the kitchen. "Peppermint tea."

I almost volunteered to take her G&T. Why not? I was back where I started in May, squarely screwed by the criminal justice system. Any day now the newspapers would call, and because a pretty white girl was involved, the national news trucks would park on our lawn and point their satellite dishes at the sky above our house and beam me around the world. That called for at least eighty proof.

Dad felt me staring at him.

"Don't you have homework?" he asked.

62.

The weird part was that my classes were getting easier now that I wasn't actually in them. My teachers were sending along assignments, notes, links to research websites and worksheets. The one thing that kept kicking my butt was English. It was hard enough writing a paper once. Mr Salvatore wanted at least three drafts, with correctly spelled words. And it didn't matter how many times I reread the definitions, I could not figure out the difference between symbols, motifs, and themes. Apparently, this was important. So important that Mr S. wrote a note on my *Faustus* essay that I should come in after school to go over it with him one more time.

At first I wasn't sure if he was serious; I mean, what if he was just going to bitch at me for an hour? But I was getting a little desperate for human contact, and I didn't think he hated me as much as some people I could name, so I went.

"Motif. Symbol. Theme."

Salvatore covered the board with the definitions and gave a million examples from our books.

I didn't want to hurt his feelings. You could tell by looking at him how into this stuff he was. And he took the time with me after school when he could have been at the gym or looking for the future Mrs Salvatore, so props for that.

But I didn't get it.

He spent every minute of that hour trying to cram stuff into the concrete block I called my head. It wasn't his fault he didn't have a jackhammer.

I put my pencil down when the late-bus announcements started. "I got to go."

"Right," he said. "Wow, it's dark already. Don't you hate how that sneaks up on you?"

"Yeah. They say it happens gradually, but I don't believe them."

"It's a conspiracy on the part of the meteorologists," he said.

"I don't think meteorologists are in charge of sunsets."

"Well, whomever, then. I wasn't very good at science." He pulled a backpack out from under his desk and started sticking his books in it. "How are you doing, Tyler?"

"I think I'm passing," I said.

"No, not that. The other stuff."

"Oh." I stacked my books. "OK, I guess."

"You don't have to lie." He set his backpack on the floor and perched on the edge of his desk. "Some of us are convinced you didn't do it, you know. It's unfair that you're being treated this way... We wish we could change that."

"Oh, well, thanks. I guess."

"I heard the police are looking at a number of suspects."

"Yeah." I stood up. "But I don't see anybody else living in suspension. Thanks, Mr S., I gotta go."

"I'll be here tomorrow."

"Cool. Happy motif or whatever."

He was chuckling as I closed the door.

My freaking locker stuck again. My jacket was in there and it was freezing out, so I fought it and kicked it. By the time I got it open and grabbed the jacket and sprinted to the front door, the late buses were gone.

Crap.

It wasn't that the walk was so long it would kill me. I just wasn't in the mood.

The car started following me a couple blocks away from school. I tried to sneak a glance over my shoulder, but the glare from the streetlights made it impossible to see who was inside. They sped up and passed me.

Four and a half blocks later, just before I turned the corner, I noticed the sound of the car doors slamming, but I didn't really notice, if you know what I mean.

The footsteps were fast and heavy.

I rounded the corner and there they were. Three guys surrounded me, their arms out. They were my size, more or less, and wearing Halloween masks. I spun around. There was no room to run.

I wanted to pee my pants.

Instead, I launched myself at the guy right in front of me. He wasn't expecting it and stepped back. Just before my fist connected with him, something covered my head. I pulled at it. It was blanket, or a piece of a blanket. It smelled like a dryer sheet.

No more time to think.

It started. Not the beating of a lifetime, not bad enough to put me in the hospital, but painful. A fist to my head, kicks to my legs. I spun around, trying to stay on my feet. One of them laughed. It sounded like Parker. I was tackled. Someone was punching my stomach. I panicked, kicked, trying to get the blanket off my head so I could breathe. He finally got off me and I puked in my mouth a little. I swallowed it.

It stopped. Just like that, it was over.

One of them said something, but all I heard was a rumble, the beginning of an avalanche. The blanket was still on my head. More rumbles. The avalanche picked up speed, momentum. I blinked, could only see the dim streetlight through the weave of the blanket.

A dark shadow moved and I flinched. Someone giggled.

The shadow came close and whispered, a familiar voice. "That's what you get for hurting my sister, you perv."

A car engine started. Doors closed. They turned up the bass.

The avalanche faded away down the mountain.

I took off the blanket. It was pink and edged with satin. I spat and hawked and spat again. I folded the blanket, tucked it under my arm, and walked home.

63.

Dark house.

Hot shower until the water ran cold.

Nothing was broken, I was sure of that. One of the advantages to being beaten up by a group of suburban jocks was that they wore sneakers, not boots. If they'd had boots on, I would have been bleeding to death from internal injuries.

I couldn't let myself think of the sound of Chip's voice in my ear, because it made me think about borrowing Dad's gun and going for a walk. I took a couple swigs of NyQuil, a bunch of ibuprofen, and slowly made my way to the kitchen.

When my parents came in from their therapy session, I was sitting at the kitchen table, watching my Lucky Charms dissolve into a bowl of milk.

Mom swooped in. "Oh my God, what happened? Who did this? Oh my God, Bill. We have to get him to a hospital. Oh, Tyler, look at your poor face."

"It's just a busted lip," I said.

"Just?" she shrieked.

She launched into a rant filled with Mom-things, asking a lot of questions and not waiting for the answers. Dad said Dad-things, which were the same as Mom-things except with a lot of swear words. I wanted to tell them to be quiet because they were making my head hurt, but my head hurt too much to say anything.

I have to admit, it felt good to have Mom fussing over me. She checked out the bruises, she studied my pupils, she called the doctor, she made me lie down on the couch in the family room, she covered me with the afghan, she did it all.

Dad stood watch in the background, as if they might come through the door any second and try again. I guess that was nice of him.

They argued about whether or not to call the police, then Mom had to leave to pick up Hannah from Mandy's house.

Dad sat in the chair across from the couch. "She's gone," he said. "Do you think this is related to what happened?"

"What do you mean, 'what happened'?"

He pursed his lips. "Do you think this has any connection to your being accused of taking those pictures?"

"Thank you for saying the word 'accused'."

"Don't start. Your mother wants you to stay calm."

I poked my fingers through the afghan. "Yeah. It was Chip and his friends."

Dad took a deep breath. "Why didn't you say that before?"

"Because we both know that Mom would insist on calling the cops. She still might, but I'm telling you right now, if she does, I saw nothing, I heard nothing, I am not going to say a word, so it's a waste of time."

"All right, calm down. I agree. There's no point in calling the police. It would just complicate things."

"Complicate."

"You know what I mean."

I cocked my head to one side. I thought I heard something far away – a plane engine, or maybe a train. Dad didn't hear anything. He was picking at the lint on the arm of the chair.

"How come Milbury hasn't fired you yet?" I asked.

"Who knows? He's doing everything he can to keep me out of the office. I have to catch a six o'clock for San Diego in the morning."

"That's another reason not to call the cops," I pointed out. "If I accuse Chip, you're hosed."

He rubbed his hand over his face once but didn't say anything.

"I'm not going to school tomorrow," I said.

"No, of course not."

"I'm getting tired of all this."

No answer.

"Dad? What am I going to do?"

"I've been thinking along those lines. About your options." He stood up and walked to the bookshelf at the end of the room. He took a handful of envelopes off a high shelf. "Your mother doesn't want me to show these to you yet." He waited while I sat up and then handed the envelopes to me.

Each one had a brochure in it. Hargrave Military Academy. Fishburne Military School. Valley Forge. Uniforms. Drill instructors. Lines of teenagers at attention. Discipline, they all promised. Integrity. Excellence.

"What are these?" I asked.

He cleared his throat. "A boarding school, a military boarding school, is a good decision. A fresh start. I've already spoken to their admissions directors, explained things—"

"Things? What things exactly?"

He kept on like I hadn't said a word. "—and they all said

you could enroll in January. It's in your best interest to enter as a second-semester junior; that will increase your college chances tremendously."

The noise grew closer. It was the avalanche, back to finish off whatever life was left clinging to the side of the mountain. Imagine a hurricane mating with a blizzard, then add gravity to the mix, and seat yourself at the bottom of it, chained in place, watching it head down the mountainside, straight at. . .

"You're sending me away."

"None of these schools are cheap, but it's a sacrifice we need to make."

I stood up too fast and had to reach for the back of the couch to keep my balance. The afghan fell to the floor. Dad stood his ground, feet planted shoulder-width apart, jaw locked in position.

"You're sending me away because I'm an embarrassment," I said. "It's easier if I'm gone. You'll keep your job. You'll save on the food bill."

He didn't say a word.

Mom's car pulled in the driveway, her headlights raking through the unlit part of the house.

"We'll discuss this later," Dad said. "I've already completed the applications. They'll be mailed off as soon as the police are willing to go on record saying you are not a suspect."

The car doors slammed outside; first Mom's, then Hannah's.

I ripped the brochures with military precision into pieces

that measured two centimeters by three centimeters. When Mom walked in, I handed them to her.

The cage match, round 32,415, started up shortly after I got into bed.

Mom fired the opening salvo. "For the love of God, Bill, can't you leave him alone for one second?"

"We have to face the reality of this, Linda. We have to deal with it."

"We agreed to wait another week. As usual, you bullied your way—"

Hannah's feet thumped up the stairs and down the hall to her room. She didn't bother checking on me. I imagine she went straight to her computer. I know for sure she cranked her music to drown out the noise downstairs.

I kept my door open to listen. Why? For the same reason you slow down when you pass a horrific car crash. You want to see the severed limbs and the blood.

I didn't need a computer or a pathetic role-playing game. Hell could be found at 623 Copeland Drive.

64.

When my eyes finally opened on Friday, it was past noon. I rolled to my side and pushed myself up to a sitting position. Sat there a while, then bit the bullet and stood up and checked the damage in the mirror.

I was bummed that the bruises weren't more dramatic. The way I felt, I should have had black-and-blue baseball-sized lumps everywhere. My bottom lip was swollen and split, crusted with dried blood, but it looked more like I had walked into a door than been jumped by three guys. There were a couple marks on my back, a few bruises trying to surface on my arms. The best evidence was a huge black mark on my right butt cheek, strategically located so I wouldn't show it to anybody.

A long shower loosened up the knots in my back and arms. I wrapped a towel around my waist and wiped the steam off the mirror so I could shave. I leaned closer to the glass. The guy in the mirror looked like somebody had wrapped his heart in barbed wire and pulled. He wasn't just a loser. He was lost, no-compass lost, don't-speak-the-language lost.

I have screwed up everything.

No, that wasn't the right way to say it.

You have screwed up everything. You have a 0.00 GPA in Life. You are a useless fuck, a waste of carbon molecules. You are the spawn of a defective sperm and a reluctant egg. You do not deserve to live.

You should die.

I put the lid down and sat on the toilet. I had never put it to myself quite that way before, but once I had, there was no avoiding it. I had been thinking about this on and off for what – four years? No, five. In seventh grade I figured if I killed myself, everybody who treated me like dirt would feel awful. I used to picture them wearing black to my funeral, being forced by their parents to look into my grave and apologize for being such jerks. They were always crying. Sometimes I'd make them throw themselves on top of my coffin and beg me for another chance.

But in seventh grade, in eighth, ninth, there had always been some hope, the ignorant feeling that things might be better the next day. *This is not the worst thing*, I'd say to myself. *You can't do it unless it's the worst thing ever.*

From the toilet I could see the top half of my face in the mirror. A guy could only hate himself so much, could only get sucker-punched a couple million times before he'd finally get the hint that maybe the world didn't want him around.

Why bother trying? What was the point? So I could go to some suck-ass college, get a diploma, march out into a job that I hated, marry a pretty girl who would want to divorce me, but then she wouldn't because we'd have kids, so instead she'd become the angry woman at the other end of the kitchen table, and the kids would grow up watching this, until one day I'd look at my son and he'd look just like that face in the bathroom mirror?

If that was life, then it was twisted.

There was only one problem left.

How.

What would achieve the goals of a) a quick death, b) a painless death, and c) a neat death? Call me weird, but I couldn't check out knowing I was leaving a nasty mess for somebody to clean up.

The gun was the obvious choice, the nine-millimeter Beretta pistol in my father's bottom drawer, wrapped in a moth-eaten red sweater that had belonged to Grandpa Miller. We weren't supposed to know it was there. We weren't supposed to know about the ammunition, either. We certainly weren't supposed to know how to load and aim it. I had done it so often I could do it in the dark.

Quick? Oh, yeah. Painless? Doubtful, but with the right aim, the pain would only last for a nanosecond. Neat? Hardly. In fact, a gun would make the biggest mess of all.

Or I could drink myself to death. The tools were downstairs in the liquor cabinet. Not quick. I didn't know about painless. If I started puking before my ticket was punched, it would be disgusting. It also presented a very not-cool exit possibility: I might get drunk enough to puke, then drown in my own vomit. Not an option.

I'd have to think about this for a while. Killing myself was the one thing I couldn't afford to screw up.

I went to my room and put on a pair of jeans and an old sweatshirt. Putting the sweatshirt on took a long time. I was hurt more than I realized. The bruises were deep and would take their own sweet time surfacing.

I made myself a plate of eggs, bacon, and toast with butter and raspberry jam, and ate while channel surfing. The only thing on was commercials. Buy our razors and be a man. Buy our pit stick and be a man. Spray this junk down your shorts

and women will crawl all over you. Get a second mortgage.
Buy a second car. Buy our razors.

I chewed through the last of the bacon and licked the
yellow strands of yolk off the plate. I chugged my juice and
wiped my mouth on my sleeve and then it hit me.

I knew the how and the where and the when.

I knew the perfect place.

65.

Eight thirty p.m.

Mom and Hannah at the mall.

Dad? California or something. Not at home – that was all
that mattered.

I was walking, me and my feet.

Me and my feet and a winter jacket, knit cap, and spare
set of keys to the doors of Washington High School, Home of
the Warriors. It was so cold that I pulled my arms out of my
jacket sleeves and shoved my frozen fingers up in my armpits.
The empty sleeves bounced like they were balloons. I reeked.
I was sweating the sharp kind of sweat that doesn't wash out.
When the coroner dissected my body, she'd notice how bad my
fingers smelled and she'd write about it in the autopsy report.
Embarrassing, yeah, but not enough to make me put my
hands into the frozen night air again.

School was open late because of basketball practice and

wrestling practice and volleyball practice, plus the stage crew was working on sets and there were lights on in a half dozen windows – those teachers who were crazy or dedicated enough to keep working at nine o'clock on a Friday night. I was willing to bet that Mr Salvatore was one of them. I should have brought a note to slip in his mailbox. Even when he was yelling at me, I could tell it was because he wanted me to do better. Or at least to learn how to spell.

As I walked in the front door, I hiked up my jacket collar, pulled down my cap, and tried to walk like I had a little bit of a load in my pants, the way the jocks did. Nobody noticed me except for two little girls who looked like they were waiting for their sister to get out of volleyball. Nobody stopped me.

I turned left, away from the activity. I knew which halls were blocked off with locked metal gates, and which halls were open so that Dopey, Toothless, and Joe could finish up their night duties without going through the hassles of locking and unlocking them. There were some advantages to having been the janitors' doughnut bitch all summer.

I worked my way up to the fourth floor without being seen. I used my key to open the door that led to the roof. It was even colder up there. Higher altitude. The wind made my eyes water.

Haloes of light pooled around the bottom of the light poles and spilled across the concrete that led to the front door. That was my landing spot, as close to the base of the flagpole as I could get. I closed my eyes to visualize: I'd take a deep breath, jump up and down a little to make the blood flow. I'd back up ten paces, take another deep breath, then sprint the final sprint, dismount, rocket through the air, fall like a comet. The end.

If I landed at the base of that flagpole, I'd be a legend. The students of Washington High would think about me every time they entered the building. They'd erect a plaque, plant flowers or a memorial tree.

But wait.

If I splatted there, one of those little kids waiting for her sister to finish volleyball practice might find my body. Talk about your bad karma. Scarring an innocent kid for life like that might be such a heinous cosmic crime, my soul would be forced back here, and I would have to relive this pathetic existence all over again. So the flagpole was out. The whole front of the building was out.

I walked to the north side. If I jumped there, I'd land in the pine trees that were growing too close to the building. I kept walking. Most of the west edge fronted the staff parking lots and the loading docks. I couldn't make Dopey, Toothless, and Joe scrape me off the pavement. They didn't deserve that. The south side was landscaped with bushes. If I landed on those, I'd be looking at broken bones, internal bleeding at best.

As I paced the roof, the practices finished and the building emptied out. My nose hairs were icicles. My fingers were numb. Freezing to death – what was the word? – hypothermia. I could just lie down and go to sleep. What could be easier than that?

It wouldn't be quick, though. In fact, it could take hours. Days even, if it warmed up enough on Saturday.

What I really needed was an ice-covered lake. A big one, the kind that you can't see across except with binoculars, like they had in Minnesota. The ice would be thick at the edges but thinner in the middle, weak enough that it would crack open if I jumped up and down a couple of times. If the water was cold enough, I'd fall "asleep" before the fear of drowning set in. My corpse would be a solid block of ice – nothing icky that would freak anyone out. They could even have an open-casket funeral if they wanted.

They probably wouldn't.

I paced back and forth, rubbing my arms. *You moron, you fool.* What kind of suicide plan was that – death by ice fishing?

A cracking metal sound made me jump. I turned around. Janitor Joe was standing under the light hung over the door.

"What are you doing here?" I asked.

"That's my question," he said.

The cold was making my nose drip. I sniffed. "I thought I'd check the seams on the patches we did."

"In August."

"Yeah, those. First time the temperature has been this low. Wouldn't want them to split, wouldn't want any leaks."

"Come over here."

I sniffed again and walked towards him. He grabbed my chin and turned it for a better look in the weak light. "You get punched in the mouth?"

I nodded. He let go of my chin.

"You don't learn so fast, do you, Miller? Didn't your old man ever teach you how to fight back?"

"No, that never came up."

He walked to the edge and looked over it.

"What are you doing?" I asked.

"Checking. Sometimes kids come up here, they throw stuff off."

"I wouldn't do that."

"I didn't think so, but it doesn't hurt to check." He walked back to me, zipping his jacket up high under his chin.

"Have you ever been to Minnesota?" I asked.

He shook his head. "Ohio is cold enough for my wife. I'd never get her to move up there." He flipped up his collar. "Is that where you're going?"

"What do you mean?"

"You always struck me as the kind of kid who runs when things get tough."

"That's not very nice."

"I'm not a nice guy. What can I say?" He shoved his hands in his pockets. "My advice? Pick someplace warmer. Texas. My wife would like Texas."

The parking lot below us filled with the echoes of friends calling to each other, car doors slamming, engines roaring to life. Somebody peeled out.

I wiped my nose on my sleeve. "If I don't go to jail, my dad is sending me to military school."

He hawked and spat into the dark. "No offense, Miller, but your father is a grade-A asshole. And no offense again, but so what? You gonna spend the rest of your days whining because your dad's a jerk? I hate people like that. Don't be a baby – live your own life."

He opened the door to the stairwell and waved me in. "Time to go home. My wife gets nervous when I'm late."

I headed down the stairs as he locked the door.

"How did you get up here anyway? You have a key?"

"No," I lied. "The door was open."

66.

I watched headlights skate across my ceiling as I turned eighteen.

Happy birthday, Tyler John.

It was magic. One minute I was a kid, then – *poof!* – next minute I was an adult. Now I could vote, and join the army, and buy lottery tickets, and get married (if I lost my mind), and make a will, and sue, and buy porn (legally), and get a tattoo, and buy guns, and go to real jail, not juvie hall, and work as many hours as I wanted.

I still couldn't drink alcohol or rent a car. The birthday fairy wasn't that clever.

In elementary school, Mom always baked cupcakes for me to take in on my birthday. She also sent a bag of grapes for the kids who were allergic. I never had a party at my house. I knew it would be a total disaster, so whenever they asked if I wanted one, I said no. Secretly, I wanted a bowling party, but I was afraid to bring it up.

You can't kill yourself. You have to run away.

Maybe I'd take myself bowling once I got to Minnesota.

You can't kill yourself. You have to run away.

67

"Mom says you shouldn't sleep all morning."

Slam. Hannah made sure my door was firmly closed.

I laid my head back down on the pillow.

She opened the door again. "Did you know that I have to babysit? Mom told Mrs Bentley I would do it without even asking me. And I'm sick." She coughed.

Slam.

She opened the door a third time. "Oh, and happy birthday. You're supposed to be a man now. That's a load of crap if you ask me, but whatever."

Slam.

The phone woke me an hour later.

"Happy birthday, Tyler."

"Thanks, Mom."

"Did Hannah get to the Bentleys'?"

"I guess so. She was pissed. Said she was sick."

"She gets sick at the most convenient times. Sit!"

"I'm still in bed, Mom."

Barking erupted on the other end of the phone. "Hold on," Mom shouted. She said something to a human, yelled at the dogs, then walked away from the noise, or the noise was dragged away from her.

"Sorry about that," she finally said.

"St Bernard?"

"A German shepherd named Kezzie and two collies. It's a blended family. They're still dealing with some pack issues."

"Why are you taking their picture?"

"For the owners' wedding invitation."

"You're kidding."

"Nope. They're trying to get veils on the collies right now. Get down, Kezzie, sit!"

Would she miss me?

That was a stupid question – of course she would. But it wouldn't be too bad, not after the first week or so. She'd stay busy with work and vacuuming and taking care of Hannah. They'd take care of each other.

"Do you have any big plans for today?" she asked.

"That's funny, Mom."

"Feeling sorry for yourself won't help," she scolded. "It's your birthday."

194

"I don't feel like it."

"Dad's in San Diego, but the three of us could go out to dinner to celebrate."

"I'd rather stay in."

"Hang on." She set the phone down on something hard and called to somebody about the veils. There was more barking and the sound of an argument breaking out, then Mom picked back up. "Thank God I'm not shooting the wedding," she muttered. "This place is a zoo."

"I guess," I said. "So, I'll see you later."

"Wait, Tyler?"

"Yeah?"

"Don't forget to bring in the garbage cans from the curb."

My mother would be fine after I left. She'd pack up my room into brown cardboard boxes. She'd fold the flaps down, secure them with duct tape, and put the boxes in the basement. After a couple years, she'd forget where she put them. A couple years after that, she'd forget she ever had the boxes in the first place.

68.

~~Dear family,~~

~~Dear Mom and Dad,~~

~~Dear mom and hannah,~~

195

Hey—
This is hard to write. Harder to say, so I'm writing. Tell
people I joined the Army

No, the navy. Since the idea started with a frozen lake, it
should be the navy. That was what Mr S. would call a motif, a
nautical motif. Damn, I finally figured it out, and it was too
late to do anything about it.

the ~~Army~~ Navy. Or I'm volunteering with
disadvantaged kids in Africa or Masachusets.
Whatever feels right. You have to stay here with them
looking at you and talking about you. I don't. I mean, I
can't. That's why I'm leaving. But tell them what you
want.

Two things: Give Yoda my computer. He can use it for
parts. I don't care who you give my clothes to. Please
tell the custodial staff that I appreciated all they did.
~~Tell Mr Salvatore I said thanks, and tell Chip~~

Blame my DNA, a bad genetic twist. It's not your
fault. Not really. Don't look for me. I'm not coming
back.

I wasn't sure how to end it: *Your Son, Truly, Love,
Sincerely, See ya* ... nothing fit. The whole letter sucked,

pathetic words that didn't come close to what I was trying to say. Plus I knew that "Massachusetts" was spelled wrong, but I couldn't figure out how to fix it. My computer was still in custody, and I didn't have the password to Hannah's, which meant I'd have to look it up the old-fashioned way.

Why bother? What if the letter became public? What if some sleazy tabloid journalist snuck in and stole it and then it was splashed all over the papers? My family would have to live not only with the shame of a screwed-up son who couldn't figure out how to make them happy, but with the knowledge that he was a terrible speller, too.

I hated to admit it, but Salvatore was right. There was no such thing as a great first draft.

It took a long time to find the dictionary in the basement. It was on the bottom shelf of Dad's bookcase, buried under accounting journals and software manuals.

Hannah was standing in my room when I opened the door, holding my note in her hand.

"Ty?"

"Why are you home?" I asked.

She shook the paper. "Are you serious? You're running away?"

"You weren't supposed to see that."

"Where are you going?"

A horn beeped from the driveway.

"Who's that?" I asked.

"Argh," Hannah muttered. She went to the window and waved. "Mrs Bentley. She offered me triple overtime to stay the rest of the day. I just came home to get my bio book. Didn't know you were going to ruin my life."

"Leave me alone." I tried to grab the note, but she kept it out of my reach.

"Leave you alone?"

"Don't scream, Hannah."

"Leave you *alone*?" Her voice pitched up another octave on the last word. The windows vibrated dangerously. "Are you nuts? No, don't answer that."

"You don't get it."

"Oh, that's right." She sat on the bed. "I don't get it because I don't live here. I don't have the same parents as you, or go to your school. I'm not going out with your best friend. I don't know anything about you."

I handed her a tissue from the box on my desk, but she wiped her nose and eyes on my pillow.

"You don't," I said.

"Shut up," she said.

"You don't know anything!"

"Please don't yell."

"Don't yell? Why not?" I yelled.

"You're scaring me." She sniffed and swallowed more tears. "How is running away going to help?"

I sat in my chair. "If they don't arrest me, Dad's sending me to military school. How's that for options?"

Mrs Bentley laid on her horn again.

Hannah threw the pillow, stalked across the room, and opened the window. "Hang on!" she screamed before slamming the window shut again. She turned to me. "I'm calling Mom."

"No, don't!"

"I'm supposed to go babysitting and let you ruin your life? Do I look that stupid?"

"Don't call Mom. It will upset her."

"You think?"

The horn sounded again, so long and loud I wondered if it had gotten stuck. It made the inside of my head wobble and my ears ring.

"I'm telling her I changed my mind," Hannah said.

I grabbed her arm. "I won't go," I lied. "I'll stay. For a couple days. We can talk, you and me, later."

"You won't go."

"I won't."

"Calvin will be home soon." She glanced at her watch. "He called me from the turnpike a little while ago. Will you go to his house?"

"Will it make you happy?"

"Of course it will, you idiot."

"I'll go."

"You swear."

"I swear," I lied. "Now go before Mrs Bentley has a fit."

69

Can't think about Hannah. Won't think about Hannah. Have to get out.

I ate a peanut-butter-and-jelly sandwich and called the train station. The first stop would be Cleveland, then I'd take a 3:20 a.m. train to Chicago, change trains one more time, and pull into St. Paul at ten thirty the next night. From there I could catch a bus to northern Minnesota. I looked it up on a map. There were hundreds of little towns. I'd get a job in a bowling alley. Rent a room above a garage, buy a space heater. I could live on ramen noodles and hot dogs.

The trip would cost a little more than $170.00. Plus food. Plus I should have some extra to get by until I found a job. This was a problem. All my money went to pay for the Foul Deed. Under normal circumstances, Yoda would loan it to me, no questions, but Hannah was probably blabbing to him that very second, so that wouldn't work.

I had to get out ASAP. If I waited, I'd be stuck. Every day would be a death of a thousand paper cuts that would close up overnight and bleed fresh the next morning. It didn't matter if they arrested me. It didn't matter where Dad sent me. If I didn't get out, I was doomed.

I ate another sandwich. Where could I get the money?

Dad.

*

Before I went up to his room, I double-checked the entire house. I couldn't shake the feeling that he was hiding somewhere, watching me. I went through the basement and the first floor, then climbed the stairs, walked the length of the hall, and slowly opened the door to his room, the master bedroom.

"Dad?"

Bed, dresser drawers, two doors – closet and bathroom. It smelled like aftershave and dust. His bed was made and the curtains were closed tight.

I walked to the bathroom. Inside was a white sink, a white toilet, and a white tub with a red plastic shower curtain crusted with dried soap scum. Prescription bottles filled with blood-pressure and cholesterol drugs were lined up like reserve soldiers on the top shelf of the medicine cabinet, above the shaving cream, deodorant, and toothpaste.

One time I stood next to him in front of this sink, and he lathered his face until it looked like a Santa beard. Before he shaved, he lathered my face, too, and gave me an old toothbrush to use as my razor. We shaved together, that time when I was too short to reach the faucets.

I closed the door of the medicine cabinet a little hard. The shelves inside screeched and fell down.

A small wooden box with unused cuff links inside sat on top of Dad's dresser, behind the bottle of aftershave and next to a large box of Kleenex. A business card from the law firm of

Hewson, Heiligman, and Keehn lay in front of the aftershave. Damn lawyers were popping up everywhere. I stuck the card in my back pocket. Found my driver's licence in the cuff link box. Snagged that, too.

I tore through his drawers looking for money and whatever else was hidden under his creased briefs and long, limp socks. He had lots of socks. He also had a couple pairs of suspenders, two ancient copies of *Playboy*, short-sleeved white undershirts, stacks of folded sweaters, and an abandoned comb. No cash.

I did not open the bottom drawer. I knew what was in there. Given that my mind was fractured into a million pieces, I wasn't going to tempt myself.

Go on. Get the money and run.

His closet was filled with clean, starched shirts bound together in groups of threes with twisty-ties and hermetically sealed in dry-cleaner bags. His suits, ten shades of black, were in dry-cleaner bags, too. I threw them on the bed to make more room in the closet. A couple slithered to the floor with plastic hisses.

He used to keep a stash of Clancy novels in here, but they were gone. I ran my hand along the top shelf, peeked in a shoe box of old photos, checked the pockets of a raincoat. *No money.* I stuck my hand in all of his shoes: loafers, scuffed dress shoes, unworn slippers, sneakers.

Jackpot. Ten fifty-dollar bills were rolled up in the toe of a left sneaker, top-quality Nikes, never worn. Four sizes too small for me. *Damn.*

I stuffed the bills in my pocket, headed for the door, then stopped.

No, I wasn't going to open the bottom drawer. No, I wasn't going to take it out, touch it, one last time. No, I wasn't going to think about it.

I couldn't help myself.

I pulled Grandpa's sweater out of the drawer carefully, carrying it in two hands. Dad kept the gun unloaded, but you never knew. When you least expected it, that was when the bang happened. I set it on the bed and removed the four boxes of ammunition from the drawer. Dad had stocked up. Must have expected a prolonged siege.

I unfolded the sweater.

A nine-millimeter Beretta pistol, weapon of champions.

The smell drifted up: machine shop and gun oil and something else, like nails or charcoal.

I reached for it.

With the clip empty, the Beretta was muzzle-heavy and tipped forward. It was designed so that a full clip would balance it properly.

I opened a box of ammunition. You had to load the bullets into the clip by hand, ten of them. This was tricky. Bullets are sly, slippery. They glide through your fingers like a feather or a strand of girl's hair, then they bounce on the carpet and hide.

I pushed the bullets, one by one, into the clip. They dropped, one by one, into place. When the clip was full, I slid it into the grip. I loaded a round into the chamber. The sound echoed off the mirror and ceiling.

With the clip locked and loaded, the gun was stabilized. It fit in my hand like a steel glove. I stood in my best cop pose, semi-crouch, on the balls of my feet, weapon gripped in a double fist. I pointed it, and *bam! bam!* pretended to shoot Dad right through the pillows.

That smell hit me again. What was it, exactly?

I brought the end of the muzzle close to my nose, sniffed. Bitter. It brushed my lips. I flinched. It smelled like a handful of coins and maybe Dad's stench, him sitting on his bed holding this pistol, sweat trickling down his neck.

The tip of my tongue did a drive-by. The gun tasted like bicycle handles and earrings and cheap scotch. I wasn't going to do it, I know, but it was here, in my hand, so easy, so close.

I wasn't going to do it, but I couldn't remember why.

I put my mouth around the end.

No.

I pulled back.

Me at the end of a rope in a dog collar, skating on a frozen pond, world watching from a shaky tree limb, waiting for me to fall through to the black water below.

204

The house was empty.

Yes.

I sat on the end of his bed, in front of the mirror. Looking back at me were rectangles intersecting rectangles intersecting rectangles – red walls, long drapes, padded headboard, burgundy pillows, beige bedspread. The pattern was ruined only by the black suits sprawled like broken wings, and my face.

I licked the barrel and closed my eyes.

I will pull this trigger and a bullet will rip through my skull at eight hundred miles an hour.

I will pull this trigger and my brains will detonate.

I will pull this trigger and fall.

No, not sitting, not sitting on his bed.

I stood up.

I stuck the gun deeper in my mouth, pointed up at the target. My hands shook, teeth chattering on the frozen barrel.

Homo, fuge.

I opened my eyes to watch it reach out for me. I wanted to see Death up close and personal. I wanted to shake His hand.

Homo, fuge.

*

I could see my legs from the knees up, my sweatshirt, my neck, chin, hand wrapped around the grip of the Beretta, but that was it. Dad had positioned the mirror on the wall for his height. I was too tall.

To watch myself die, I'd have to hunch over a little.

I was bigger than my father.

I pulled the gun out of my mouth. The barrel was wet. My teeth ached like I had been chewing on aluminum foil.

I didn't fit.

I was a different size, a different shape. I kept trying to squeeze into a body, a skin suit, that was too small. It rubbed me the wrong way. I blistered. I callused. I scarred over and it kept hurting. I would never fit.

But, really, I didn't want to fit. That's why it was hard.

I put the gun on the dresser next to the Kleenex box, muzzle pointing away from me.

My knees suddenly gave out and my stomach flipped. I staggered to the bathroom and puked my sandwiches into his toilet.

I flushed. Rinsed my mouth.

Stuck my head in the sink and ran cold water over it. My ears filled with water and then my brain, and my nose and mouth, but this was the opposite of drowning, this was coming out of the water back into the world.

I shut off the faucet and combed my hair with my fingers. The water ran down my face and neck and down my back, but it wasn't cold at all. It was electric.

I grabbed the gun and the boxes of bullets before I left his room. I went down the hall and dug out my baseball bat, too.

70.

I'm not sure how I got to Yoda's. Maybe I teleported. One second I was at my house, next second – *poof!* – I was at his, heavy backpack over my shoulder, bat in my hand, finger stabbing at the bell.

He opened the door wearing a Case Western shirt. He had a lollipop in his mouth.

I raised my hands. "Don't say anything. Just listen."

He moved the lollipop to the other cheek.

"You were right. I was a total asshole at the mall. I apologize. I'm sorry." I slid the backpack off my shoulder and set it on the ground. "I'm having the worst day of my life. I know it's lame to do this – apologizing, then asking for a favour – but I need a ride."

He removed the lollipop. "Where are we going?"

The pitching machine released the ball – *thunk*. I swung – *whiff*. Another ball – *thunk*. Another swing – *whiff*.

"I thought the point of this was to actually hit the ball," Yoda said.

"I'm warming up," I said, shuffling my feet on the mat and crouching low in the batter's cage. My centre of balance had shifted when I walked out of Dad's room. It was throwing everything off.

Thunk. Whiff.

"Is that what it's called?" he asked.

We were in the white inflated dome of Action Sports, the place down the street from the mall where you could shag baseballs, shoot hoops, play pool or arcade games, and drink overpriced soda from ten in the morning to ten at night. Five bucks rented me the cage and batting helmet, and I could get ten pitches for two dollars by sticking tokens into the machine to the left of home plate.

Yoda studied the guys in the other cages. "Why don't you try swinging like them?" he suggested.

"I have my own swing, thank you very much."

Thunk. Whiff.

"Yeah. I can see how that's working for you. Why can't you just play a video-game version? That way you could be comfortably sitting on a couch."

"It's not the same," I said, missing another ball. My shoulders were sore and my ribs were talking to me. I was batting barehanded, with a gun waiting in the car and more than four hundred dollars in my pocket. I was starting to sweat. Plus, my gut ached from puking and my head was spinning. The blisters were rising quickly.

Thunk. Whiff.

"What are you trying to hit?" Yoda asked.

"The small white ball flying towards my head at seventy-five miles an hour."

"No, see, that's your problem," he said. "You're dealing in reality, not metaphor. Hannah's coach makes the team visualize attacking someone before a game begins. Who do you want to beat up?"

"Chip Milbury," I spat out. *Thunk.* The ball rocketed towards the plate. My arms twitched and the bat swung, catching the ball on the tip and swatting it away with a hollow *ping*.

"See? It's already working," he said. "It's a Force thing."

"Don't start." The ball flew out of the tube and past my bat, crashing into the net behind me.

"Concentrate, you should. Visualize."

Thunk.

Chip, again, his head like a watermelon on a picnic table, my bat swinging through it, pink juice and black seeds exploding.

Thwack.

"Good hit," Yoda said.

Thunk.

Bethany, I couldn't hit her, not with a bat, but I could tell her off, walk up to her at tennis practice or her locker and say, "Sorry, there, Beth, but you lost big-time. I would have been the boyfriend you always wanted, the good guy. And you blew it."

Thwack.

"Wow," Yoda said. "That was far."

Mr Milbury and his wrinkled Barbie-doll wife and their breakable champagne glasses and their tacky fountain and their—

"You missed," Yoda pointed out.

"Do you mind?" I wiped my forehead on my sleeve. "I'm trying to concentrate here."

He folded his arms over his chest. "Sorry."

"Thank you." I plunked in two more tokens and dialled up the pitching speed.

"Shouldn't you be slowing it down to increase your chances of hitting the ball?"

"The faster it comes in, the faster it goes out," I said.

The first ball blew by before I was in my stance, but I was ready for the second, *thwack*, the third, *thwack*, and then I found my balance and fell into an easy rhythm, *thwack*, wait, *thwack*, wait.

I became an armed beast roaming the streets of a helpless suburb, crushing cars and buses, destroying buildings with a single swing, *thwack*. I wiped out the football stadium, *thwack*. I annihilated Josh Rawson's party, *thwack*. I destroyed every jerk who had ever looked at me sideways, and *thwack*, the courthouse, *thwack*, the judge and my P.O., and *thwack*, my father, *thwack*, *thwack*, *thwack*, every bone in his body snapping like kindling wood.

The balls stopped coming. Yoda looked up at me. "Done yet?"

71.

Yoda talked the whole way to the river, but I couldn't hear him. It felt like an oversized batting helmet was on my head, like the ear holes weren't lined up, and the brim dipped over my eyes.

"Turn here," I finally said.

Yoda turned into the park entrance and slowed down for the speed bump.

"Go all the way to the end," I said. "Then take the left."

When we turned into the parking lot that fronted on the river, I pointed to the farthest row of the spaces, where the gravel bled into the grass, ten feet from the edge of the riverbank. He parked and we got out. The wind had picked up, blowing the empty swings on the playground back and forth, and making small whitecaps. We were the only people there.

"That is some nasty water," Yoda said.

"Chemical plant upstream."

"Does this have anything to do with you running away?" he asked.

"She told you?"

"I just hung up with her when you rang the bell."

A Big Gulp cup floated by. I grabbed the backpack. "This won't take long."

He followed me to the water's edge. "What are you doing?"

I unzipped the pack, took out a box of ammunition, and poured a handful of bullets. I brought my arm back and threw them as hard as I could. They sailed in an arc, then dropped fast and hit the water with heavy *plop-plop-plop*s.

Yoda's eyes bugged. "Jesus God, Tyler! You are throwing bullets into the river."

I threw another handful. "Observant, you are," I said.

"Where did you get them?"

"My father." Another handful.

"Wait. Stop. The metal is bad for the fish."

"They're not going to blow up." I paused and looked at the oily foam collected in the weeds. "Do you really think there are fish in there?"

"Maybe not now, but bullets won't exactly welcome them."

"I can't throw them in the garbage can. What if a kid finds them, or they blow up the dump truck when they get compacted?"

"We can Google it at my house. There has to be an approved method for bullet disposal."

"Can I throw the gun in?"

Yoda grabbed at his knit cap with both hands. "The *gun*? You have a *gun*? What in the hell is going on?"

I pulled the Beretta out of the backpack. "This won't hurt the fish," I said. "And if I take it apart" – I ejected the clip and removed the barrel – "it can't hurt anybody."

I threw the clip and the barrel north, and pitched the grip south. When I threw the grip, I could feel it in my sore ribs and my shoulder. Yoda watched with me as the metal pieces slammed into the water and were swallowed.

My eyes started leaking and my nose, too. I let my hair fall in front of my face and looked down at my hands.

"You OK?" he asked.

I nodded my head and wiped my eyes. "Guns are dangerous."

"Yeah. That's what they say."

I turned my hands over. The blisters from the batting cage burned on my fingers and palms. My calluses from the summer were a memory. I bit the biggest blister and water poured out.

Yoda looked in the backpack. "Do you have any grenades in there?"

"Nope. That's it."

He picked up the pack and slung it over his shoulder. "It took forty-seven strikes before you hit a ball today."

"Forty-seven?"

"I counted."

"Ah."

We walked to the car. I put the backpack between my legs and buckled my seat belt. He started the engine.

"Forty-seven?" I asked. "You sure?"

"Yep."

"That's a lot."

"I wasn't going to say anything." He checked the mirror and backed out, then put it in drive.

There were four virgin blisters on my left hand and five on my right, plus the popped one. A blister is a defense mechanism, Mr Pirelli explained on my first day of work. He told me to keep them clean and bandaged and remember to use gloves the next time.

I bit at the blisters, popping all of them open, and rubbed them on my jeans. It felt like my hands were on fire.

"What are you doing?" Yoda asked. "Won't those get infected?"

I flexed my fingers. "Calluses build up faster this way."

72.

I went to bed at ten o'clock and slept for thirteen hours.

Spent all of Sunday catching up on homework. I read *Faustus* again and the passages of *Paradise Lost* that Salvatore hinted would be on the next test. Wrote an essay about the aftermath of the Three-Fifths Compromise. Conjugated future conditional irregular verbs in French. Did calc until numbers oozed out of my ears. I even did an art history assignment – studied pictures from the early Renaissance and wrote a reaction piece. I had to define "renaissance." At first I wrote "gathering of military intelligence, like for a raid." Then I looked it up in the dictionary. Renaissance meant "rebirth" and was "a revival of culture and learning." The other word I was thinking of was "reconnaissance." An understandable mistake.

While I studied, Mom and Hannah glided around the house like shadows I could barely see or hear. Dad wouldn't be home until Monday night. After dinner.

The temperature dropped twenty degrees by sunset and the wind howled from the north. Shingles flapped on the roof.

73.

I woke up in a sweat, tasting metal in my mouth. I panicked, grabbed the edge of my mattress, and tried to remember what I had done with the gun. The fog lifted in my brain: *No, I don't have it. No, I didn't do it.* My lip had split open again in the night. There was a little blood on my pillow. I felt better after I brushed my teeth.

I drove Yoda's car to school so he and Hannah could snuggle in the backseat. Riding shotgun were my backpack and a large plastic garbage bag, tied at the top. I would not tell them what was in the bag. Yoda squeezed it and was relieved that it was soft.

I turned the key in the ignition. The engine sputtered,

then caught, and I pressed the accelerator. The engine roared, instant boner. My hands sweated as I gripped the steering wheel. Time to drive, my licence in my wallet glowing like plutonium. Tyler Miller, Lord of the Universe. I revved it one more time, redlining the tachometer.

"Hey," Yoda called from the back. "Stop it. You trying to blow a gasket?"

I put it in gear and drove off, keeping to all posted speed limits.

I did not go to my cell for homeroom. I went right to Hughes's office. His secretary said he'd be in meetings until third period and suggested I wait for him in my personal Siberia.

"Sorry, I can't," I said. "I have a couple of appointments. I'll be back."

The guidance counsellor wasn't expecting me, either. I looked through some college catalogues while I waited and ripped out a few pages that looked promising. When she let me in, I shook her hand and explained what I wanted. She looked at me over the tops of her glasses and said one word. "Impossible."

"Please check my date of birth on your computer."

Her fingers clicked on the keys. "Oh. Happy birthday."

"Thank you."

"But you still need parental signatures to do this. District rules."

"No problem," I nodded. "You get the papers together and I'll make sure they get signed. And can you give me a hall pass?"

I gave all the homework I'd done on Sunday to the secretary so she could put it in my teachers' boxes just as Hughes came in, his face red. He rifled through his phone messages and told me to follow him into his office.

"Two hours wasted just so they could tell us we're getting even less federal funding next year." He took off his coat and put it on a hanger. "I didn't think it was possible to get less federal funding, but there you go." As he put his coat in the closet, he muttered something about "jackass mandates" that I couldn't quite hear.

He sat at his desk, glanced at his monitor, and finally looked at me. "Have a seat."

"No, thanks. I'll stand."

"Suit yourself. What's the problem?"

Deep breath, deep breath, just like you planned it.

"It's not really a problem. I thought I'd give you a heads-up. I'm changing my schedule for next semester." I put my hands behind my back so he couldn't see them shaking. "I'll get my parents to sign off on it tonight."

"Oh?"

"Yes. And starting tomorrow, I'll be attending all of my classes."

"But we agreed—"

Deep breath.

"That was a dumb thing for me to do. I wasn't thinking straight. Now I am. I'm going to all of my classes tomorrow. You should tell your spies and the security people. If I get hurt, if I get punched or knocked down, or harassed more than the average student, I will contact the school board and the newspaper. I'm not the problem here, Mr Hughes. I'm tired of feeling like I am."

I stopped at the custodian's office on my way to the cafeteria and handed Joe my keys. While he jiggled them in his hands, I apologized for stealing them.

"Apology accepted," he finally said.

"If the judge gives me more community service, can I do it with you?" I asked.

He nodded. "No problem." He locked the keys in his desk drawer. "But if you ever take anything from me again, I'll kick your ass."

"Understood."

The cafeteria was at full volume when I walked in. Feeding time at the monkey house.

A few people watched as I passed the table where Yoda and Hannah sat. More noticed when I stopped in front of the table occupied by Chip and his minions, along with Bethany and a few of her underfed friends.

"Get out of here," Chip said.

"Not yet." I tossed the big plastic bag at him. He grabbed it before it landed on his tray.

"What's this?"

"I thought your mother might want it back," I said.

A low "Oooooohhhhhhh" started at neighbouring tables. Chip stood up as Bethany untied the bag and pulled out the pink blanket with the satin edge.

"That's what you threw over my head the night you beat me up," I said. "Parker" – I pointed at him – "you were there, but I still can't figure out who the third guy was. Austin? Jordie?"

All eyes focused on Chip. "Get out before I flatten you."

I turned to the kids behind me. "Did you hear what he said?" A couple heads nodded.

"Anytime, anyplace, Chippie," I said.

He came around the end of the table and stood six inches away from me.

"Right here, right now, loser," he said.

Please hit me, please hit me, please hit me, go on, take a swing.

"Bravo, very good," I said. "Ask me to fight in the room that has the most security." I pointed to the cafeteria monitors staring at us.

"You think you can take me?" He shoved his chest forward like he was trying to show me his cleavage.

Just throw the first punch, Chippie, I'm begging.

"You know I can. I let you win at your party. You were too scared to take me on in the locker room. When you finally got

219

around to it last week, you needed two henchmen and a blankie. How pathetic is that?"

Out of the corner of my eye I could see a security guard walking towards us, and Bethany in a furious conversation with Parker, who looked like he wanted to hide in the mashed potatoes.

"A real man faces his conflicts, Chippie. On his own."

I started to walk away, then stopped and backed up.

"Just in case you decide to go crying to Daddy because I had the balls to talk to you?" I flicked the card from Hewson, Heiligman, and Keehn so that it landed in the middle of the table. "Tell him to call my lawyer."

The security guard walked me to the guidance counsellor's office so I could pick up my paperwork, then to the attendance office so I could sign out, then to the front door. That was nice of him.

As I approached the wall of doors that faced the flagpole, I saw Bethany's reflection in the glass. She was running towards us, carrying the pink blanket.

"Tyler!" she called.

I hesitated, my shoulder against the door.

"I want to talk to you," she said, pouting, hands on her hips. "I mean, I think we should talk."

I smiled at her reflection, pushed open the door, and left.

One more loose end.

Since I didn't have an appointment, the secretary at the

courthouse said I'd have to wait an hour before Mr Benson could see me. While I was waiting, I called Pirelli Landscaping and left a message saying I could work weekends again, if Mr Pirelli was interested.

My stomach gurgled. I hadn't eaten anything at lunch and I was feeling sick from all that homework the night before. The taste of the Beretta was still in my mouth and nose, lurking in the background. I put three sticks of gum in my mouth and pulled a *Highlights* magazine from the stack on the table. I used to love going to the dentist so I could read it.

I kept one hand curled around the edge of the chair to keep me steady. I wasn't on thin ice any more, but everything still felt slippery. There was a chance I was going to fall flat on my face. But I had to keep moving.

Mr Benson did not flash his possum teeth when I was finally ushered into his office. I explained I was trying to take control of a few things, and I wanted to know what was going to happen to my probation because of the party violations.

"Assuming you're not arrested?" he asked, leaning back in his chair.

"Yes, assuming that."

He put his hands behind his head and asked me questions about school and life and attitude and girlfriends and just about everything except for the kind of underwear I wore. I didn't think it would be so complicated, but I answered everything and tried not to sweat.

He finally set the front legs of the chair back on the floor. "If they let you off the hook for the camera thing, no charges at all, I'll recommend six more months' probation and community service. The judge will probably accept my recommendations. What do you think?"

"Sounds fair. Can I work with the janitors again?"

"Don't see why not." He stood up.

I did the same and reached out to shake his hand. "Thank you, sir."

"Pleasure's all mine."

The day had unfolded precisely the way I'd planned.

The bus showed up at the corner just as I left the courthouse. I got a seat that didn't smell funny. An abandoned newspaper was on the seat next to me. When I read about a car crash, I did not imagine myself going through the windshield. When I read about a fire, I didn't feel the flames.

I was a boy on a bus going somewhere, for a change.

The walk from the bus stop to Yoda's house took ten minutes. His parents had just gone grocery shopping, and their pantry was packed with snacks and soda. We took a couple armloads to the basement, where I spent the afternoon kicking his butt in an empire far, far away.

It was the perfect day right up until the hysterical phone call from my mother.

74

It didn't matter how many times I saw it, a police car in my driveway always gave me a jolt.

Mom jumped off the living-room couch and threw herself at me, hugging hard enough to fracture my ribs. Her mascara was running in two black crayon streaks down her face. I patted her on the back, tried to breathe, and looked around for my sister. She wasn't there. Officer Adams was. He studied the shine on his shoes and the cobwebs strung along the crown moulding as we waited for her to finish.

Mom pulled away with a loud gulp. "I'm sorry," she said. "I didn't realize how scared I was until just this moment." She smoothed the mascara stains on my shirt.

"Have a seat," Adams suggested. "I'm sure you have a lot of questions."

Mom sat on the couch.

I stayed on my feet. "What's going on?"

Adams cleared his throat. "We arrested a student from Forestdale this morning for all the crimes associated with the photographs taken of Bethany Milbury."

"What's his name?"

"I can't tell you. He's sixteen."

Mom puddled up again and snagged a Kleenex out of the box on the end table.

"Why him?" I asked.

"We received a couple tips about his behaviour at the party.

Our computer guys were able to trace the original upload of the pictures to an account paid for by the suspect's grandmother. The grandmother is loaded and we've been fencing with her lawyers all week. But we have all the evidence we need now. He's going to do time, no question about it."

The words rippled over me.

"I apologize for any inconvenience," Adams said, "but we had to perform a thorough investigation."

"Tyler?" Mom asked. "Honey, are you OK?"

"You're sure," I repeated. "You're not going to come back next week and say you changed your mind?"

Adams explained the whole thing again. He added that he had emailed the school administrators, and he would follow up with a phone call to Mr Hughes in the morning.

"My deputy is putting your computer back in your room right now," he said. "If you have any problems with it, don't hesitate to give our office a call." He stood up and straightened the creases on his pants. "I imagine you're relieved. I'm just sorry we couldn't clear this up any faster."

They looked at me. It was my turn to speak or burst into tears. Show some gratitude, at least. I didn't feel grateful. I just felt tall.

The deputy came down the stairs, Hannah close behind. Adams stood up. "You'll need to call your PO this week."

"Already did," I said. "I met with him this afternoon."

Adams nodded. "I'll make sure his office gets the paperwork. Sorry again for the inconvenience."

"When will Dad be home?" I asked as the cop car pulled out of sight.

"His plane landed an hour ago," Mom said. "He had an emergency meeting with Brice. Do you want Chinese or pizza?"

Something hit the house just as Mom, Hannah, and I were about to dig into a stress-free, MSG-enhanced meal in the family room with Alex Trebek. Mom had lit fat, white candles for atmosphere, the soda cans were popped open, and the soy sauce was poured.

A car turned into the driveway going too fast. There was the squeal of brakes and a slight thud, which turned out to be Dad's car hitting the back wall of the garage. The house shook again seconds later when he slammed the door. He made it to the family room in six quick strides. He stopped when he saw me at the end of the couch.

"You sonuvabitch."

My heart lurched, but I forced myself to slurp up the strands of my lo mein. "Look who's home."

His jacket and tie were missing, his top two buttons unbuttoned. There were sweat stains under his arms. His eyes were bloodshot and his comb-over looked like a squirrel had run through it.

Mom shook her head. "Tyler, hush."

Dad swayed and put his hand on the wall to balance himself. "You little bastard."

I opened another packet of soy sauce and poured it on my noodles. "Those names insult Mom, not me. Want to try again?"

Hannah gasped.

"That's it." He started across the carpet for me.

I wait until he's in arm's reach. I wait until he hits me, until he's off balance and unprepared. I punch him square in the middle of his body. I collapse his lungs and stop his heart. He drops to the ground.

I stood up.

"No, Bill, no!" Mom shrieked as she stepped between us and grabbed Dad. "What are you doing?"

"Proud of yourself?" he asked over Mom's shoulder. "You finally stuck it to me."

"I don't know what you're talking about."

"Milbury fired me. He's blaming me for Nebraska. He wants to sacrifice me to the Feds. But we both know the real story, don't we, Tyler John?"

"You've been drinking, Bill," Mom said. "Please calm down."

"Shut up, Linda."

As the words hit, Mom's head snapped up and her chin jutted forward.

I pick him up by the throat and lift him slowly until his

feet dangle three inches from the floor. He can't make a
sound. His fingers claw desperately at my hands. His feet
kick. I squeeze.

Mom let go of Dad and walked over to stand next to Hannah, in arm's reach of the fireplace pokers. "The police were here," she said. "They arrested the boy who took those pictures. Tyler is completely innocent."

"What?" He cocked his head to one side.

"It's over," Mom said. "The whole thing." She filled him in on what the police told us, her voice like glass.

Dad paused, his forehead wrinkled with effort. "You're sure this isn't a trick?"

"Disappointed?" I asked.

He smoothed his hairs over the top of his scalp, trying to line them up between his fingers. "That doesn't change anything. Your shenanigans cost me my job. That means no money, no college, no house."

"I don't understand," Hannah said. "How did Tyler get you fired?"

"He threatened to beat the crap out of Milbury's son at school today. There are twenty witnesses. He's obsessed with that family."

I scratched my chin. My beard was beginning to grow in faster. "Wrong," I told him. "You were fired because you screwed up, or maybe you're a scapegoat, but it wasn't me."

"Enough!" Dad's arm hit the closest TV tray. Three containers of food flew through the air and smacked the wall with a wet sound, the candlelight glittering like tracer fire before it was put out in the duck sauce. Mom's cheeks were flecked with black drops of soy. Hannah whimpered.

Dad spun on his heel and disappeared down the stairs to the basement.

Alex Trebek told us to stay tuned.

Hannah helped Mom sit down on the couch, then picked up the remote and turned off the television. "Why did you have to make it worse?" she asked me. "You could have just let him calm down."

I picked a napkin off the floor, sat down next to Mom, and wiped the gunk off her face.

"Are you OK?" I asked.

"He's under a lot of stress." She took the napkin from me. "We all are." She walked over to the mess on the floor. "Let's pick this up. Oh, no, there's wax on the carpet."

While Hannah and I picked up the remains of dinner, Mom twisted an ice-cube tray in the kitchen. The sound of the ice cracking echoed off the appliances and tile like a gunshot. It made me jump. She came in carrying the ice in one hand, and two twenty-dollar bills in the other.

"I want you to go to the movies," she said. "Tyler, you can drive the van. Your licence is in the box on your father's bureau."

"I know."

Hannah interrupted. "Aren't you coming with us?"

"I have a headache," Mom said. "I'm going to rest. That way your father will have a quiet house."

Hannah said something soothing about Tylenol and a cold compress.

My hands itched. The open blisters were on fire. The heat spread up my arms, across my shoulders, and down my body like sheets of flame that welded all my bits and pieces together. I looked down at the carpet, half expecting to see it melt under my feet. The table lamps seemed to have new bulbs in them, clean bulbs that highlighted the grease spots on the wall, every line in my mother's face, and the nervous glances that Hannah sent to the basement door. Their shadows were stark.

Hannah pretended to smile as she buried Mom's money deep in the pocket of her jeans. Mom crouched and put the ice on the wax stuck to the carpet.

"This is bullshit," I blurted out.

"What?" Mom asked.

"Why can't we admit what's going on here? Sending us to the movies, pretending you just need a nap – it's all bullshit. Covering up for him makes it worse."

"Don't, Ty," Hannah said.

"We're all just trying to get through this," Mom said.

"That's not good enough," I said. "Not any more."

*

I crossed the room and opened the basement door and walked down the first three steps.

"No one is to come down here," roared William T. Miller.

I retreated up the stairs to the kitchen, reached in the front hall closet, and took out my baseball bat. Without looking at my mother, I adjusted my armor and headed back down.

75.

It was dark down there, but I could see him in the recliner, his shoes off, his headphones already on, and music flowing through them. He had not touched his computer.

I flicked on the overhead lights.

His eyes opened. "I need to be alone, Tyler."

I walked past the recliner to the bookcase that held his stereo equipment, crouched down, and unplugged the receiver.

Dad rocked the recliner forward and threw his headphones to the ground. "Don't push me."

I stood up. "I want to talk."

"Put the bat down."

"Forget it."

His eyes widened. "Excuse me?"

"You heard me. You're not going to scream and intimidate me. Not today, Dad."

The hand holding the bat was sweating.

Mom crept down the stairs, afraid of what she would find at the bottom. "Is everything OK?"

"Leave us alone, Linda," Dad said.

I leaned against the door that led to the storage room, my left hand resting on the table covered with the dusty train set. Santa was still riding high. The mountaintop was dirty.

"This'll only take a minute," I said. "She should stay."

Mom's eyes ran back and forth between Dad and me, then she slowly sank down and sat on the third step from the bottom.

Dad's eyes narrowed. "You have two seconds."

"Give him a chance, Bill," Mom said.

"This is between him and me, Linda. Be quiet."

My heart pounded double-time, a hammer beating on the inside of my ribs. My mouth went dry. Adrenaline surged, screaming through my brain, begging me to take him down.

A red haze filtered over everything, like a light rain.

"I'm a part of this," Mom insisted.

"Go upstairs," Dad told her.

"Shut up." I said it calmly, the way you might say "looks like rain" or "the mail's here".

Mom drew in a little breath and hugged herself.

"What did you just say?" Dad stepped towards me, wings unfolding.

"I told you to shut up."

"How dare you?" Dad spat. "You ungrateful—"

"Bill, can't you see what's going on?" Mom pleaded.

"Shut up, shut up, shut up!" Dad yelled, his fists balled tight.

There was a *click*, a faint *click* that I felt more than I heard.

Something snapped.

I picked up the bat. I brought it up in a perfect arc to achieve maximum velocity and force, then smashed it into the model train set, sending Santa plunging down the mountain and exploding the pretend world.

Thwack, thwack, thwack, thwack.

One, two, three, four.

Mom screamed.

Dad grabbed at my arms.

Thwack, thwack, thwack, thwack.

The temporary rivets holding me together loosened, glowing hot under the pressure that prevented me from turning the bat on my father and breaking it over his head until he was a pile of splintered bone and broken track, beating him until the wheels came off. I hit the train table harder so I wouldn't hit him.

Mom screamed again and Hannah was there, and Dad finally stepped back and I stopped.

All I could hear was my breath coming fast, hard, and loud, like I was underwater and wearing an oxygen mask connected to a heavy tank strapped on my back, and the only sound that could fit in my head was the rasping air going in and out of my lungs.

I set the bat down carefully at my feet, lifted my head, and pushed the hair out of my face. I was soaked, as if I had just walked through a storm.

I took another deep breath. Other sounds filtered in: Mom patting Hannah's back, Hannah trying not to cry, Dad saying, "It's okay, it's okay, Tyler, calm down, it's OK."

The red haze lifted. I licked my lips. I wiped my hands on my jeans. The open blisters burned.

"I'm going to talk now," I said.

My father nodded once.

"Please sit down."

Dad sat on the edge of his recliner. His black socks drooped around his ankles. Mom and Hannah retreated to the foot of the stairs, their eyes darting between my father and me.

"Thank you," I said. I emptied my pockets and handed $480.00 in bills to him.

"That's your money," I said. "I stole it from your closet on Saturday. I spent twenty bucks hitting balls."

Dad's face was stone. "You were in my room?"

"I needed money to go to Minnesota."

"What?" Mom whispered.

"I hear it's nice there. I figured it would be a good place to start out on my own."

The furnace kicked on.

"Will you get me a garbage can?" I asked my sister. "The black one in the garage. And call Yoda. Tell him I'm coming back."

Hannah had a puzzled look on her face, but she went upstairs. I took a deep, slow breath, waiting for her to get out of earshot.

"What made you stay?" Mom asked.

"Dad's gun."

"You touched my gun?" He gripped the chair. "Why—?"

"I asked you to shut up."

Mom started to cry. I couldn't look at her, because if I did I might fall apart, and Dad would take control again and it would be the same as before, only worse. I crouched next to the train wreck and picked up the broken engine. "I didn't really want to run away. I wanted to die."

I turned the engine over and over in my hands. The smokestack and wheels had snapped off, but the body was whole.

"But you didn't do it," Dad said.

I opened my mouth. I knew my voice was going to crack. I cleared my throat and waited.

Dad didn't know what to do with his hands. He rubbed them once on his thighs; he crossed his arms over his chest and immediately uncrossed them. He kept his eyes on a carpet stain six inches to the left of me.

I tried again. "I had the gun in my mouth and my finger on the trigger."

Mom cried silently, rocking back and forth.

Dad flinched but quickly recovered. "What stopped you?"

"I looked in the mirror and realized that I was already dead. I let you kill me one piece at a time, starting when I was, what? Eight years old? Nine? You killed yourself and then you came after us."

My eyes were leaking again. *Damn.* I wiped them on my sleeve.

"I never hit you." Dad's voice shook. "I sacrificed everything to give you a good life and a nice home, something better than I had."

"You're a real success story, Mr Miller. You got the big house, but nobody lives here. Not really. Anyway." I tossed the engine on the trash heap. "So. I'm not dead. I'm not going to be dead for a long time, I hope."

"Are you blaming me for this?" Dad asked.

I let the question hang there, spinning. Mom was crying raw sobs, gulping for air. Dad looked smaller than he had five minutes earlier, like the air was being let out through a small, hidden puncture.

"Do I blame you?" The words came out slowly. "Absolutely. You loaded the gun and put it in my hand. I blame myself, too. I let you do it." I stood up and brushed off my hands. "I am not going to military school. And I'm dropping most of my AP classes."

"What?" Dad sputtered.

"If you don't agree, I'll drop out."

"If you drop out, you can't live here." His voice was higher, wobbly. More air was rushing out of him, his cheeks hollow, his skin beginning to collapse.

"Fine. I figure you won't pay for college, either. No problems. You did it, Dad. How hard can it be?"

Hannah came down the stairs holding the garbage can. I took it from her and set it next to the disaster site.

"What's going on?" she asked.

"Dad has to clean up his mess," I said.

76.

I ate dinner at Yoda's house. His parents had cooked turkey meat loaf and beet salad and squash. It was no wonder Yoda was the way he was.

I ate everything they put in front of me and drank three glasses of milk. Yoda and his parents talked about Case Western Reserve University and if it really was a better choice than Ohio State. Every time Mrs Hodges asked me if I was feeling well, I did the polite thing and lied.

Yoda explained what was going on when I was in the bathroom. When I came back to the table, his mother said she thought it would be best if I stayed the night.

*

After dinner, we sat in the family room, and I watched his father watch the news for a while, then Yoda and I went down to his room with a box of chocolate-chip cookies. He turned the television to one of the music video channels and muted it.

"I've been thinking about your problem," he said.

"You make it sound like a skin condition," I said.

"You need another option."

"Besides running away or beating my father to death?"

"Exactly."

"Damn." I put two cookies in my mouth.

"You could stay here," he said.

"Until graduation? I don't think so."

"Why not? My parents like you – they think you're a good influence."

I snorted cookie crumbs and coughed. "Wait until they get to know me better."

"You can't afford an apartment."

"I know. There's always the army or the navy."

"Funny," Yoda said.

"Ha," I said.

I stuffed more cookies in my mouth. Yoda did the same thing. We chewed our cud, watching booties and boobs and fat rappers getting out of slick cars.

"You forgot to mention that I could gut it out at home," I said. "I do happen to live there. And who knows? Maybe I'll get lucky and they'll arrest my dad for whatever happened in Omaha."

"It could happen," Yoda said. "Pigs could fly out of my butt, too. You never know."

I slept on his couch, under a pile of afghans. I passed out after midnight and slept like death until just before seven, when the sound of Yoda's snoring nearly caused the walls to cave in.

It took a couple minutes to figure out where I was and why I was there. Once I oriented myself, I lay back down and pulled the afghans up under my chin.

I was chilled, but it felt like I had a sunburn, the kind that hurts but itches at the same time, and you can't stop yourself from scratching even though you know it's going to hurt worse. My hands ached, my shoulders were sore, and my stomach was killing me, either from the cookies or from everything else. There was no way to get comfortable.

The sky around the edges of the curtains was pale.

I got up and put my clothes on, folded the afghans, and scribbled a note that I put in the centre of Yoda's keyboard. I went up the stairs holding my sneakers, staying on the edges of the treads so they wouldn't squeak. I made it out the door without a sound.

77.

It was warmer than I thought it would be, and bright enough to make me squint. I left my jacket open.

The street smelled strangely of tar, which made me worry that maybe I was hallucinating.

I turned the corner and saw that the street crew was repairing a couple of potholes that had grown large enough to swallow tyres whole. The tar smelled like summer, even though everything around me looked like fall dying into winter.

I was going to walk past my house to see if it was still standing. I felt like the game-winning runner on third base, waiting for the signal to sprint home and dive headfirst – one part nervous excitement, nine parts nausea. It was finally beginning to sink in what I had done.

Mom would let me take my clothes, that was a given. The computer would be harder, but if I had to get by using the computer in the library, I could do it. At the very least I had to get my Social Security card and my passport, and I needed my textbooks, something to read, and my boots, for when it snowed.

I had been watching the sidewalk, looking for the heaves and cracks that send you landing on your face, so I didn't look up at the house until I turned in the driveway.

He was sitting on the front steps. He was wearing the same clothes that he had come home in the night before, except he had sneakers on, and the beige comforter from his bed was wrapped around his shoulders.

The road crew's truck beeped a high-pitched warning as it backed up. Crows roosting in the maple tree called back.

"Hello," he said.

I watched. Listened.

"I wondered if you would come back." He tugged on the comforter. "Wondered all night, in fact."

"Did Mom kick you out?" I asked.

"No. She thought about it, talked about it, but she went to sleep. I couldn't. Couldn't sleep, I mean."

I watched.

He shifted closer to the railing. "Will you sit next to me?"

The truck stopped backing up and beeping.

"OK." I sat. The concrete was a slab of ice under my butt.

"Do you want to sit on this?" he asked, offering the blanket.

"I'm fine," I said.

We both stared straight ahead. A television would have been nice, something we could pretend to look at, but all we had was a lawn gone dormant for the winter and a street awaiting pothole repairs.

"My father beat me with his belt a couple times a week for my entire childhood," he said. "That's why I swore I'd never hit you or your sister. And I never did."

"No, you didn't."

"But it wasn't enough."

I picked at the edge of a popped blister. "No," I said quietly. "It's not."

He rubbed his hand along his sandpaper beard stubble. "I'm sorry."

I held my breath.

"I thought I was different than he was."

The road crew poured hot tar and asphalt into the cracks in the road and tamped it down.

"Are they going to arrest you?" I asked.

"At work? I don't know. I have to get a lawyer."

"Good idea."

The crew filled the hole at the bottom of our driveway.

"Your sister said you slept at Calvin's last night."

I nodded.

"That was nice of them."

"They're nice people. We had meat loaf."

"Meat loaf is nice."

"Yeah."

When the crew moved down the road, Dad stood up. "Are you hungry?"

We both poured bowls of cereal. Dad started the coffeemaker and made toast. He put butter on his toast and mine. I added raspberry jam.

We sat down facing each other and ate in silence, except for the slurps of milk on the spoon and the crunch of toast. We took turns studying the backyard out the window and examining the grain of the wood in the kitchen table. When I was finished eating, I carried my bowl and plate to the dishwasher and put them in.

"Did you get enough?" he asked.

"I'm still kind of hungry," I admitted.

"I could fry some eggs," he offered.

"I can do it myself," I said.

He sipped the last of his coffee.

"Do you want a couple?" I asked.

He blinked. "Yes, that would be nice. Sunny side up."

"I know."

I opened the refrigerator door and took out the egg carton. When I turned back to the stove, he was standing in front of me, his eyes wet and lost.

"I don't want you to leave us." His throat tightened and he clenched his teeth.

I put the egg carton on the counter.

"I don't know what I'm supposed to say." He coughed once. "I'm bad at this. I'm sorry." He fought for control, the muscles along his jaw rippling. "I will try to do it better. Everything. I'll try."

I put my arms around him. He pulled me close, hugging me back. He groaned, an agonized sound from deep inside, and I worried that maybe he was having a stroke, but he didn't let go. I did. I let myself break apart and lean all of my weight on him. He held me closer and patted my back like I was a little kid, whispering to me, until we both felt like we could stand on our own.

He wiped the tears off my face.

I did the same for him.

*

242

We ate eggs, bacon, sausage, and Pop-Tarts, and polished off the orange juice. We talked a little, but not too much.

I brought in the paper and handed him the business section. I read sports and the comics. Then we traded.

78.

Dad didn't go down into the basement after breakfast. Progress. He fell asleep on the couch with the newspaper on his stomach.

Mom and Hannah tried to make a big deal out of me being home, but I asked them to stop, so they did. Mom took over the kitchen table to go through the real-estate listings and watch Dad out of the corner of her eye. Hannah went to Yoda's house.

I played Tophet to empty my brain and numb everything else. Gormley grew stronger exponentially, and I scored an obscene amount of spellpoints and kills. By dinnertime, I had finally made it: Level One.

I put the game on pause long enough to inhale a stack of grilled-cheese sandwiches and tell Mom that yes, everything was fine, I just had a lot of work to do on the computer.

The confrontation with the Lord of Darkness was thirty-seven minutes of mad skills and sick mayhem.

I won. I beat the game.

And then a new screen, one I had never seen before, never even heard of, popped up.

It gave me a choice. I could become the new Lord of Darkness myself, or I could take a gamble and be reincarnated.

I chose wisely.

Acknowledgements

Writing a novel sometimes feels like riding a roller coaster.

No, that's a lie.

Writing a novel *always* feels like riding a roller coaster, the kind that makes you hyperventilate, say your prayers, and regret the cheese dog you ate half an hour ago. Once they lock you in your seat, you're sure you will plunge to a fiery, painful death. When it's over, you sprint to get back in line, because it was the coolest thing you ever did.

The following brave souls took turns strapping themselves in next to me for this ride.

I owe them all big-time.

My friends, Deborah Heiligman, Martha Hewson, and Elizabeth Bleicher all read early drafts of the book and insisted I keep going. Special thanks to Martha for staging the semicolon intervention.

Our kids are the most patient people on the planet. Thank you, Stephanie, for reading the book before I had written the ending, and then not killing me when I admitted I didn't know what happened next. Thank you, Meredith, for saying *exactly* the right thing when I needed to hear it. And thank you, Jessica and Christian, for putting up with me when I wandered the house muttering to myself.

My first husband, Greg, goes above and beyond the duties of a former spouse. Not only is he a good friend and father, but he is my secret weapon in the war against grammar mistakes. Many thanks to him for taking the time to read this, armed with a red pen.

My parents, Joyce and Frank Halse, watched the revision process of this book up close and personal and never once reminded me that I should have taken that typing class in high school. They're sweet like that.

The best bookstore in the country, The River's End Bookstore in Oswego, New York has a magic chair in it. Thank you, thank you, Mindy Ostrow and Bill Reilly for letting me write the opening pages of my books in that chair.

I am very fortunate to work with the talented people at Writers House. Many thanks to my agent, Amy Berkower, who makes it possible for me to ride roller coasters all year long. Genevieve Gagne-Hawes took the time to read an early draft and offered insightful and much appreciated comments. Becca Stumpf is an organizational genius, and is always cheerful and polite, despite working in New York City.

Deep bows to my editor, Sharyn November, who rode with me through all the plunges, corkscrew turns, loop-de-loops, and soaring climbs to the sky. I hope your stomach has finally settled. Thank you also to the other ab-fab folks *chez* Penguin Group: Doug Whiteman, Regina Hayes, Eileen Bishop Kreit, and all of the creative people whose hard work made this book possible. I am very grateful to have my books supported by a company that has both integrity and a sense of humour.

I could not have written this book without the companionship of my beloved husband, Scot. He was always there cheering from the sidelines, patting my hand, and brewing endless gallons of tea and coffee. Every time I started crumbling around the edges, he was there to sweep up the pieces and put me together again.

I don't have enough words to thank all of the guys, including Mike, Mike, Ted, Marshall, Steve, Dan, various marching-band players (you know who you are), David, Jared, Jordan, and the hundreds of others who talked to me in their schools and wrote to tell me what their truth was. This book is in no way based on any of the stories they shared, but I hope it echoes and reflects their struggles and triumphs.